A Kelly Society Christmas

by

S.K. Andrews

The Kelly Society, Book 2

A Kelly Society Christmas

COPYRIGHT © 2022 by S.K. Andrews

Cover Art by *Debbie Taylor*

The Wild Rose Press, Inc.
PO Box 708
Adams Basin, NY 14410-0708
Visit us at www.thewildrosepress.com

Publishing History
First Edition, 2022
Trade Paperback ISBN 978-1-5092-4267-2
Digital ISBN 978-1-5092-4268-9

The Kelly Society, Book 2
Published in the United States of America

Vivien picked up her petticoats with one hand, clung to her songbook with the other, and ran. "Josh, Brian, come with us! We have to stay together!" she called over her shoulder.

Neal held onto his top hat and ran alongside Vivien.

A group of four millennials whipped their heads around and started following Krampus, Vivien, and Neal.

"Wow! This show is dope!"

"Don't you know who that is?" The red-haired woman in their group pointed her finger. "That's Krampus! My cousin went to the Krampusnacht Festival in Austria last year. He's the opposite of Santa Claus. He's a Christmas demon who punishes naughty children!"

"Let's go!"

"Yeah, let's check it out!"

They crossed the street with hollers and laughter.

To her horror, Vivien glanced back to see a mass of individuals pacing behind them in the middle of the road. The caroling team, Christmas shoppers, and random folks holding coffee cups moved in to see what would happen.

Dedication

A Kelly Society Christmas is dedicated to the real Patsy Carroll, my aunt Patricia Kellems. She is known to us as Aunt Pat, who has the passion of Ireland and the strength of the Lower East Side, New York. I speak for my entire family when I say, "We love you Aunt Pat!"

Chapter One

Vivien Kelly bolted up in bed gasping. Her fingers gripped the puffy white comforter so tightly, she created a ball of the bedspread. Slowly, Vivien recognized her own bedroom bathed in early morning sunlight and lingering shadows. Her eyes gratefully took in French doors leading to her second-floor balcony, an eggshell tableau mantelpiece above the hearth, and her small Queen Anne style walnut bureau with brass handles inherited from her mother.

Neal stirred awake next to her. He pulled Vivien close as worry clouded his sea green eyes.

Finally catching her breath, Vivien rested her head upon his bare chest.

Neal's soothing voice nuzzled in her ear. "Another nightmare?"

She nodded.

"What was it, honey? A banshee? A shadow creature? One of those evil black-eyed children?"

"No," Vivien answered on a shaky exhale. "I dreamt it was Christmas morning, and I hadn't bought any gifts."

After a few seconds Neal's guffaws bellowed through the bedroom.

"This is no laughing matter!" Vivien slapped his arm.

Neal shifted and pulled her back at arm's length.

"Have you forgotten what you did yesterday morning before the crack of dawn?"

"I know, but…"

"No buts. You stood on that cliff and decapitated a demon who already covered our planet in dark clouds and commanded banshees to torment humans. If you hadn't killed Dagda, none of us would be here to anticipate Christmas. You literally saved the modern world." He stroked Vivien's long chocolate brown hair. "I'm honored to have such a badass warrior woman as my girlfriend."

Vivien laughed softly and sighed. "It is bizarre to think that happened just twenty-four hours ago."

"You should rest today." Neal gazed into her emerald green eyes and kissed her temple. Then he plopped his head back on a fluffy white pillow.

Vivien rose halfway out of bed to glance down at him. "Actually, I need to do my Christmas shopping. I have to go."

"Can we have five more minutes of down time?"

Vivien ran her fingers through his reddish-brown hair, slightly longer behind the ears due to a lack of sitting in a barber's chair. Self-grooming had been the last thing on Neal's mind the past month while the woman he loved prepared to fight a powerful Celtic demon. He gave her a charming smile, and Vivien's skin tingled with joy.

"Okay. Five minutes."

"Come here." Neal pulled her into a tender embrace.

After only three minutes, Vivien rose again. "Sorry, hon, but I've got to get to Hillsdale mall. With holiday hours in effect the stores open at eight o'clock.

If I get ready now, I can be among the first inside." After sliding off the bed, Vivien moved about the room. "Some of my favorite places are right here in Half Moon Bay, like Posh Moon and Tokenz, but the bulk of what I want is at the mall. At least I don't have to drive into San Francisco, which saves me two hours round trip." A satisfied sigh escaped her throat. "Everything I need is close by."

"Are you sure you should be out and about? You got five stitches in your arm just yesterday. Can't you take one day off?" Neal pleaded, leaning upon one elbow and rubbing his eyes.

After a quick perusal of a gauze bandage wrapped around her forearm, Vivien shrugged. She yanked a bra and panties out of her top drawer and ran around, trying to peel out of a black lace negligée. "Neal! Today is December twenty-second! You seem to forget you've done all your holiday purchases. You distracted yourself the past two days with mad shopping. As for me, I couldn't do anything but train my body and focus on defeating that disgusting demon!" She thrust her right leg into a pair of jeans, almost falling over.

"I love watching you dress." Leaning his head back, Neal tempted her with a sexy smile.

"Oh, shut up!" When Vivien hurled her negligée at him through laughter, it covered his face.

After pulling the nightgown off his forehead, Neal sniffed the satin material with a grin. "Smells good."

Chuckling, Vivien tugged into a large sweater the color of cranberries. Then, she reached for her grandmother's silver holly bell pin sitting in an open jewelry box. She wore it every holiday season. Four inches long in every direction, the brooch consisted of three silver holly leaves surrounding a miniature silver bell, which jingled every time she moved a certain way. Vivien found the perfect spot for her Christmas adornment and then secured the tiny lock on the back. Gazing at her reflection in the mirror with the pin just below her left shoulder made her smile. Vivien tapped the bell lightly, and a sweet chiming sound arose. "There."

Leaning against the four poster California King, Vivien held out her hand. "Give me that."

Instead of handing over the sexy black nightie, Neal pulled her down into a passionate embrace.

Vivien let go, kissing her soulmate with all her heart. Finally, she pressed her palm against his chest, drawing back. "Seriously, I have to leave."

A seductive smile occupied Neal's handsome face again as he patted the mattress. "Stay here for a few more hours."

"No way!" Vivien snatched her negligée and then flung her body from the bed.

Neal groaned and finally got up. "All right, then. I'm going to make some coffee."

She stopped moving. "Really? That's so sweet of you, honey. Now I can add a spot of makeup before I go. I'll still get to the stores early enough." Vivien slid her negligée into a dresser drawer and took a seat at her vanity.

Neal hastily dressed in a pair of jeans and a beige Half Moon Bay Surf Company T-shirt. "I'll meet you downstairs."

"Okay." Vivien replied, as she opened a small drawer packed with makeup.

****

Neal checked two client emails on his phone while Vivien's snazzy Italian coffee maker emitted a rich maple and herbal aroma from her Christmas blend. She'd bought four bags from Java Hut coffee house the previous afternoon.

It seemed strange to think about delivering blueprints by mid-January after the world nearly ended. Neal contemplated his design of two homes being built on the cliffs ten miles up the coastline. Habit told him to give each client a summary of his progress, but for now, he simply typed "Happy holidays and we'll touch base after the new year." With that, Neal sent off each email and put down the phone.

He arched back and let out a big sigh. After gazing out Vivien's backyard windows for a long moment, Neal's head dropped into his hands.

"I have to tell her."

That sentence would not leave Neal's brain. When he riveted awake from a past-life dream six months ago, he knew this time would come. In the dream, gazing upon his reflection as a prominent Roman general named Gaius Marcus Antonius from 60 A.D. shocked him to the core. A strong chiseled face stared back, framed by black hair, complete with a gold chest plate over red material ending just before his knees, and dangling from his waist—a matching gold helmet.

After Neal awakened that morning watching the sunrise, he finally accepted his soul journey. Neal's current life became poetic, in a way. As Gaius, he loved Boudicca, Celtic warrior queen, but in that ancient time they stood as enemies. Even in the dream, Neal knew Vivien had been Boudicca, and now they came full circle. They enjoyed authentic love for each other. The pain had gone. Boudicca died in battle and so had he. But yesterday, they won the fight against the ancient Celtic demon standing side by side.

Glancing out the window again, he found morning sunshine caressing a rounded patch of grass and a tall eucalyptus tree. Long avocado green leaves clung to thin branches when a strong gust of wind struck. The swishing sound reassured.

"I promised myself to tell her who I was in a past life," he whispered. "The battle is over, so now I have no excuse. I need to tell her I was Gaius." Neal continued, speaking to the backyard.

He crossed his arms and turned around. After Vivien opened up and told him about her life as Boudicca centuries ago, Neal remained silent. He regretted waiting so long. But he couldn't add to Vivien's state of affairs while she prepped to kill a demon.

"Okay…right after she gets her coffee, I'll reveal my dream." Neal grinned.

He looked up in appreciation of Vivien's open kitchen design, even though he'd seen it many times. A wrought iron chandelier hung in a square above a custom white tiled kitchen counter. Next to a state-of-the-art stainless steel refrigerator, pine cupboard framed glass doors presented flower-painted white plates and mugs.

Pounding of boots on the staircase stopped Neal's thoughts.

Vivien rounded the corner juggling her black and white purse, a black wool jacket, and car keys.

"See you in ten hours, honey, if I haven't been chewed to pieces by the scariest predators of all—

Christmas shoppers!" She gave him a peck on the lips and pulled a silver travel coffee canister from the cupboard.

"Wait. I have a mug all ready for you. Sit down for a few minutes. You'll have plenty of time to shop." Not waiting for an answer, Neal poured steaming hot coffee into a white snowman mug. He turned and extended the brew to Vivien. "I made Christmas blend."

Vivien cocked her head. "Okay, I guess you're right." She tossed down the keys and bag and then draped her coat upon a kitchen counter stool. Vivien took the mug. "It smells heavenly."

Neal gestured to the tiled counter. "We've got hazelnut creamer. Or do you want peppermint mocha, gingerbread latte, or Christmas cinnamon?" He pointed to the refrigerator. "We have those too."

Setting down her coffee, Vivien opened the fridge and glanced inside. She presented Neal with a happy smirk. "You memorized the creamers?"

"Of course! It's very important. From now till New Year's Day, we are all things Christmas!" Neal laughed heartily and swept Vivien into a classic movie moment kiss.

She chuckled with joy. "I love hearing that, and I love you."

"I love you too, honey. Now sweeten up your coffee before you accuse me of making you late again."

Tinkling laughter emerged from Vivien's throat. "Yes, once again you are right." She went directly to her mug and created the perfect hazelnut Christmas blend.

Neal grabbed another snowman cup from the collection sitting on a red tray and poured himself coffee. He leaned toward Vivien, now seated on the stool across the counter. Neal opened his mouth, but nothing came out.

Vivien smiled with a squint. "You want to tell me something, don't you?"

He gazed into Vivien's emerald eyes for a few seconds. *How can I do this right now as she's rushing off to Christmas shop?* Neal realized the timing was not right.

"Actually, I'm surprised you don't already know."

"People like me don't pick up everything. For some reason this is something you'll have to tell me." Her eyes got big and round in anticipation.

Neal's phone rang. He hesitated.

"Do you have a new contractor? I think that's him and it's important." Vivien rambled off just before gulping down her coffee.

"Oh, yeah!" Neal snatched his phone from the counter behind him. "I told him to call me this week."

Vivien gathered up her coat, purse, and keys. "I need to go anyway. We can talk later." She raced down the hallway.

"Okay, good luck in the shops!" Neal chuckled before answering his phone. "Hi, Bill."

After the conversation with Bill ended, Neal once again gazed upon Vivien's serene backyard and made a final decision.

"I'll tell her on Christmas morning."

Neal let out a happy sigh as he raised the coffee mug to his lips.

Chapter Two

Josh parked six feet from the cliff's edge above a stunning shoreline. Gazing out his windshield, he eyed two seagulls hanging in midair above rolling white surf. Josh leaned his arms upon the steering wheel. He cherished the first seconds of arriving for a surf session; feeling as if the waves beckoned him.

"You okay?" his friend Brian mumbled in the passenger seat.

Josh sat up straight and glanced at Brian. "Yeah. I just love the waves, you know?"

Brian laughed. "Yeah, I know. Now let's see if the waves love us." He opened the car door.

Josh did the same and hurled himself out of the driver's seat. "We'll need to be quick. I have to be at Java Hut by noon, and I can't be late. I got in trouble before, and it took me a long time to make barista." He ran to the back of the large station wagon, unlocked two side swinging doors, and reached for his wetsuit. Sucking in fresh salty air and enjoying the sound of pounding waves reaching shore, Josh planted himself on the fender.

Brian released tie down straps atop their surfboards on the roof rack and spoke over his shoulder. "I wouldn't be afraid of being late to work. I'd be more afraid of what your dad would do if he knew you drove his 1942 classically restored Woodie onto the State

Beach parking lot." Brian joined Josh behind the car and stood with hands out, looking down. "This is all dirt! My dad would kill me! Don't you want to graduate high school intact?"

Josh laughed. "We'll be careful."

The beautiful Chrysler Town and Country Woodie appeared to glow even under filtered morning sunlight. Josh's father proclaimed to have a favorite of the Woodie genre whenever he parked for auto shows. Fans constantly took photos when they passed by. They admired elegantly arched tan wood paneled clamshell doors in the rear, flawless cobalt blue paint, silver chrome fenders, whitewall tires, a wooden slat roof rack, a sliding rear seat, and a middle seat that folded out for extra passengers, all in gorgeous two-tone wood.

"Besides, I didn't have a choice." Josh rolled down dark blue foamy fabric and stuck his leg inside, then tugged it upward. "If I want to be invited to the Mavericks Challenge one day, I have to keep practicing. My dad knows my car is in the shop." Flicking back blond hair, Josh then tossed his right arm toward the waves rolling in. "We've got to be the best we can be."

Brian snatched up his own black wetsuit and sat down next to Josh. "Yeah, you're right." As he rolled the rubber up his body, he sent Josh a sideways glance. "Hey, do you have the receipt from yesterday? I owe you for those baseball caps you bought for my cousins. I have the money now. I can pay you back."

"You can catch me tomorrow," Josh mumbled with a shrug.

"No, dude. Let's do it now. Once I get home my mom puts me on Christmas chore duty till New

Year's!"

"All right." Retrieving his wallet from the glove compartment, Josh plopped down again and filed through crinkled papers sticking out of tan leather. Pulling one out, he scanned the receipt "Oh, shit."

"What?"

"They never charged me for the Christmas fairy doll I bought my little sister. It should have set off an alarm when I went out the door, right?" Josh's anxious-looking face swiveled toward his friend.

Brian's brows wrinkled. "Yeah, it should have done that. Wait, how did you even get through check out?"

"I remember I left it on the bottom rack of the shopping cart. I must have forgotten to pull it out for the cashier."

"Crap, man! You have to take it back and pay for it."

After concentrating on the slip of paper again, Josh jammed it back into his wallet. "I'll go after work. I have to get the doll out of my mom's closet. I hope she hasn't wrapped it yet. Anyway, you owe me twenty dollars."

Brian grabbed a slim black wallet he'd set down on the silver fender and produced a twenty-dollar bill. "Here, but you better not forget to do that after your shift."

"No worries. At least I'm honest. I could have kept quiet." His eyebrows lifted, and his blue eyes sparkled as if he were up to no good.

Standing to grab the cord attached to his back zipper, Brian grinned. "No, man. Bad karma."

All zipped in and with rubber clinging to their

bodies, the aspiring surfers put their wallets and phones safely in the glove compartment. Josh locked up the car after pulling their surfboards down from the roof rack. Then, he quickly attached the car key to the interior cord of his neoprene suit.

"Dude, you trust that? What if you rip your leg against a rock or something?"

Josh winked with a sly smile. "It's all good." Then his voice dropped to a whisper, so as not to alert surfers one car away also prepping for their session on the water. "My dad has a special hide a key underneath the passenger side that's impossible to find. Only he and I know where it is, not even my mom."

Brian chuckled.

Seaweed stench invaded their nostrils upon marching down a ten-foot-high bluff. A massive blob of musty brown kelp washed up two yards down the beach and now attracted flies. Finally, the well-worn footpath landed them onto stony sand.

Picking up the pace, they jogged toward shore balancing their boards on one side.

Josh pointed. "Great swells. Okay, let's do this."

"Wait, I need to stretch for a minute." Brian laid his board down, shook out his dirty-blond hair, and extended his arms.

Streams of yellow sunlight broke through cloud cover.

"All right." Josh, the taller of the two, set down his longer board and arched his back. After observing a surfer catch a wave, he stopped. "Is that Fred?"

"Yeah."

After a few seconds, they took in an intense breath.

"Oh, no!" Josh's hands covered his face.

Brian shook his head from side to side. "Wipeout!"

"He's okay, right?" Josh lowered his hands with a confident smile.

"Yeah, he's okay." Brian snickered. "See, he's right there."

Josh pulled his board up. "C'mon."

The two surfers trotted toward the water, but Josh halted abruptly. He gazed toward the parking lot above them.

"What is it?"

Focused on the cliffs with slits for eyes, Josh mumbled, "I thought I heard a bear growling."

"What?" Brian barely got out through laughter.

Sand rumbled beneath their feet, and a fierce howl blasted through them.

"*BAD CHILDREN!*"

The teens swiveled sharply, almost knocking their boards together in the action.

Brian shivered. "Did you hear that?"

"Yeah," Josh whispered hoarsely.

Dark clouds descended, stuffing whatever sunshine remained into an invisible pocket.

All at once, chunks of the bluff above them exploded.

"It's an avalanche!" Brian yelled out.

Crashing through sandy rubble onto the beach, an eight-foot-tall, hooded figure roared. Then, one of the arms of the cape reached out to the boys.

In the blink of an eye, Josh's body transported. He now stood before the sinister entity. Josh's surfboard dropped in the sand with a thud. What he saw could not be believed, and how the hell did he get so close to this thing?

13

Two black twisting horns three feet high protruded through a filthy crimson velvet cape. A looming hood with dirty white fur lining covered the monster's head. His breath stank of sulfur and rotted flesh. Leathery cocoa-colored skin pulled across his oddly shaped face, and an unnaturally long mouth hung open. Sunken black eyes quickly dragged humans to their demise if gazed upon too long, and thick, claw-like fingers ending in ten-inch nails hung from his sleeves.

A hairy, matted goat hoof pounded into grains of sand, sending them in every direction.

Josh gazed down in what felt like slow motion, while he took in a giant hairy body with animal legs. The creature was indeed half man, half goat. But, as Josh's mind raced and his head flew up again to stare into those soulless eyes, the word "Demon" flickered into his brain like a neon sign.

Finally, Brian ran up, sans surfboard, and tried to catch his breath. "Jesus!"

"No…he's a demon," Josh uttered.

"How do you know?"

"My boss's friend Vivien banishes them. I heard them talking about it in the back office one day."

Brian faced Josh in amazed wonder. "No shit!"

One long, hideous fingernail jutted into Josh's face.

Both teens screamed, knocked back to the reality of their situation.

As the monster's heavy, stinking breath filled the air, his voice came out like a low rumbling just before an earthquake.

"You are a bad child and a thief! You fled with a Christmas fairy doll!"

Stillness hung between them like a guillotine about

to drop.

"Harvey, give it up! You're an idiot, but that's a great prank."

"Shut up, Brian. It's not Harvey."

Chuckles erupted from Brian as he doubled over. "Oh, come on!" When he moved his hand inside the monster's robe, Brian's body suddenly jettisoned into the ocean just beyond the wave break line.

"Leave him alone!" Josh pleaded.

The Christmas demon jerked his arm back from the task of tossing Brian into the sea and refocused.

Josh secured all the courage he had inside, even though his legs shook. "Look, I don't know what your name is, but I've heard of you. You find bad children and punish them during the holidays." He threw his hands up. "But you've got to listen to me, please! I didn't know the doll wasn't paid for. I'm returning it today, and I promise to pay the bill!"

That unnatural mouth curved into a wide, chilling smile revealing rows of razor-sharp teeth. "The deed is done. You are mine!" With a flick of his robe, a gigantic black sack materialized.

The demon's claws elongated, wrapped around Josh's body, and hauled him into the bag.

"No!" Josh bellowed as loud as he could, not knowing if anyone could hear him.

Chapter Three

While an instrumental version of "Winter Wonderland" played through piped-in speakers, Vivien pushed a red plastic cart. Chattering shoppers refused to move out of her way, yet Vivien hummed along to her favorite Christmas song with a smile.

Upon turning into another aisle, Vivien abruptly halted. A woman with a unibrow in a neon green running suit studied a beautiful doll she'd plucked off the shelf.

Even though the toy existed in a box, clear plastic revealed her image. At twelve inches long with a snow-white fabric body, a gorgeous pixie face, wings accented in baby blue and light pink, with ivory satin ballet slippers on her feet, the doll stood to be every young girl's fantasy Christmas present.

Vivien came up alongside the lady, transfixed on the box she held. Peering over her shoulder, intense whispers suddenly issued from Vivien's lips. "Christmas fairy doll…Christmas fairy doll…Christmas fairy doll."

"Excuse me?" The customer scrutinized Vivien with a crinkled face.

Vivien's hands snatched the box from the woman with unnatural speed. Her words transformed into a psychotic chant.

"Christmas fairy doll! Christmas fairy doll!

Christmas fairy doll!"

Backing away, the unibrow pointed at Vivien. "Lady, you are crazy!" Almost tripping over a toy robot display, the woman utilized her jogging outfit and ran away.

Vivien leaned her head against the toy box and closed her eyes. Like a sped-up movie playing in her mind, she lived Josh's terrifying dilemma. Her vision began from the moment he grasped the fairy doll, to his body thrusting into a creature's sack meant to plunge him into hell.

With no time to lose, Vivien attempted something she'd never tried before.

I am now on the beach with Josh. I am now on the beach with Josh.

Vivien laser-focused on the beach, Josh's body in front of her, and whatever demon threatened him. The retail surroundings flickered around her once, twice, and finally fell away.

All at once, Vivien's arms penetrated a see-through cosmic barrier that crackled with little lightning strikes when her fingers passed through. She was shocked and delighted as Vivien's hands latched onto Josh's shoulders. Josh's skin and bones were evident under his wetsuit. Vivien yanked him backward and felt both of them fall to the ground.

Josh scrambled up from the sandy beach where Vivien now lay. He reached down to help her.

Taking his hand, Vivien accepted a new reality— she existed in two places at once. Her body stood in that retail store, but Vivien's spirit, somehow solid, stood with Josh.

His eyes enlarged as Josh looked Vivien up and

down. The truth of what he gazed upon clicked in. "Wait a minute! How…How did you get here?"

Deep roars blew sand everywhere when the demon sprang at them.

"Don't worry about that now. Get behind me!" Vivien barked, leaping in front of Josh's body.

Vivien's hands raised high with fingers spread as far as possible. She drew upon power from every cell in her body. A solid yet clear wall she'd created held the creature back, but it would not last long.

Krampus.

Once his name entered Vivien's awareness a memory took over.

A twelve-year-old Vivien sat in front of the fireplace in her family's New York City brownstone reading a book titled *Creatures in Mythology.* After turning a page, the younger version of herself gazed upon a disturbingly hideous image. Reading in curiosity, little Vivien discovered the demon Krampus in Norse mythology existed as the son of Hel, goddess of death. According to folklore, his mother reigned over the lower realm, which had been broken into nine worlds. Krampus's purpose came to him long ago— gather up naughty children every fifth of December and drag them down to his section of hell, literally, his mother's namesake.

In a snap, Vivien came back to the current moment. "You are Krampus, are you not?" she demanded in a surprisingly calm tone, while the monster faced her only ten inches away.

Krampus lowered his massive ugly head. Sneering chuckles moved the ground beneath their feet. "I am."

"Then why are you here now? I studied you years

ago, and I know you only come out on the fifth of December."

Sunken black holes for eyes gazed into hers. "If I am here on the wrong date, you have only yourself to blame. Your winter solstice banishment of evil from this world opened a door for me."

Anger raged through Vivien like a fire out of control. "I did not allow you into my world!"

"What made you think it be you?" the disgusting entity whispered back.

Vivien's mind raced.

The flash of raw energy I felt right after killing Dagda was not my imagination.

New insight ended abruptly when Krampus's claw broke through her psychic wall.

"Run, Josh! Meet me at Java Hut!"

After Josh was out of the way, the monster's claws seized Vivien by the neck. His mighty arms swung her feet inches off the ground. *If he kills me here, will my body die in the store?* The thought filled Vivien with assurance he could not slay her, albeit short lived. She wasn't willing to take that chance.

Even though her voice came out in choking gasps, Vivien began a magical Celtic Triad chant to incapacitate Krampus.

"You created this torment. Your body shall lie dormant. For this boy is only bait, and now you must wait!"

Freed of his slimy talons, her feet landed on solid sand. Vivien bent over with hands on her thighs. After a few coughs and luxurious inhales, she straightened.

Krampus shook his head in confusion, for Vivien recited her Triad as if she were his mother, the goddess

Hel herself. After all, he made a grave mistake and must pay for his false accusation of an innocent boy.

The monster snapped his head around, peering into Vivien's soul with fury. He had been duped. Krampus charged with a deafening roar.

"Okay, so that didn't work." When Vivien threw hands up against Krampus, her fingers flickered in and out. Gazing down, she found her entire body flashing like a strobe light. The astral projection mojo faltered. Having never done this before, Vivien had no idea how long it would last.

Beyond Krampus lay an enormous piece of driftwood the size of a log. It would do damage if wielded the right way. Although Krampus stood as a powerful demon, he existed within a flesh and bone body. He could be injured.

Vivien willed herself to remain solid and threw out her arms. Instantly, the chunk of wood hoisted high into the air and pummeled down onto the creature's head.

The demon Santa Claus fell with a great thump.

She lifted her arms once more. The nearby mound of seaweed pulled apart and wrapped itself around Krampus, completely covering his ugly body.

"Holy shit!"

Vivien turned sharply. "Josh, what are you doing here? I told you to go to Java Hut."

"I couldn't leave you alone with that thing."

Placing a hand on his shoulder, Vivien smiled. "Well, thank you for that." Suddenly her brows furrowed. "But you still could have been hurt." Vivien turned back to Krampus and angled her head. "Does that look like a mass of seaweed to you?"

Josh crossed his arms over his chest. "Yep, that's

exactly what it looks like." He smirked back at Vivien. "You're amazing. I didn't know you could move things around."

Vivien's eyes went wide. "Please keep this to yourself Josh, because it's not something I want getting out."

"No problem." He chuckled.

"Why aren't you more shocked?"

Josh lifted his shoulders. "I always knew you were different."

"Gee, thanks!"

"And I overheard you and Ron talking in the back office at Java Hut one day." He blushed.

A swimmer emerged from the waves.

"Brian!" Josh hugged his friend, who breathed heavily but appeared unscathed.

"Man, what a weird morning," Brian wheezed out as he leaned over.

Josh tossed his arm toward Vivien. "Brian, this is Vivien. The paranormal cleanser I told you about."

Brian lifted one hand. "Hey."

Suddenly, a dark shadow thrust out of Krampus's body and flew above them.

Vivien reached out to the teens. "Group hug. Right now!"

In an instant they wrapped their arms around one another. Vivien silently recited a protection Triad, and the shadow dissipated. Then, she broke off their connection. "Okay, my gut is telling me Krampus will be passed out until twilight, at least his physical form. I will deal with him when he awakes. But in the meantime, I have no control of his spirit. I've just given us some protection, but you guys need to leave now and meet me at Java Hut." She stared them down with arms akimbo. "Do I make myself perfectly clear?"

Josh bobbed his head up and down. "Yeah, but I have to drop off my dad's car at my house, or I'll really be in trouble."

Vivien's face wrinkled in confusion. "Huh?"

Brian slapped Josh on the back. "No worries. We'll meet you. Josh lives close to Java Hut, so we'll walk over."

Vivien's body flashed out of sight upon her last sentence. "See you soon!"

She left the surfers with their mouths gaping open.

****

CRASH

Vivien's legs couldn't hold her speeding soul reentering a solid human body. Everything went black as Vivien's arms and limbs bumped along a hard surface. When her eyes popped open, Vivien found her body strewn upon the toy department floor.

A group of four shoppers stared down at her.

Before they could speak, Vivien leapt to her feet. She tossed the Christmas fairy doll into her cart and pushed past them.

"I'm fine! I just slipped. Merry Christmas!"

Chapter Four

In Java Hut's back office, Patsy Carroll opened her journal of recipes. She twirled back and forth in Ron's ergonomic chair reviewing her newest creation. To avoid a post-Christmas slump in sales, Patsy came up with muffin recipes to entice the breakfast crowd. While it proved to be busy in the front, her assistant manager Mary had matters well in hand. So, after jumping in for a few hours behind the counter, Patsy allowed herself to brainstorm a winter menu.

As Patsy searched her creative baking mind for a new idea, her eyes wandered around the office. Surprisingly, the small, square room appeared tidy. She sat in front of an antique rolltop desk, which Ron inherited from his grandmother. It occurred to her his respect for the desk may be why it stood free of unnecessary sticky notes and paper balls. Patsy smiled at that thought. She never expected to entertain romantic feelings for the man who hired her six months ago to manage his coffee house. It felt wonderful and scary at the same time. Dropping her journal and pen, Patsy kneaded her temples and exhaled a long breath. Since she loved her job and all her fellow employees, Patsy reminded herself to tread with caution. Even though she could swear, at times, Ron looked at her with more than just a friendly countenance.

Another smile appeared upon her face.

Picking up her journal with one hand, Patsy reached for her favorite Java Hut coffee mug with the other. She sipped dark roast brew with her standard cream and one sugar. Patsy's suggestion to add a coffee maker to the staff break room was met with gratitude from Ron. Now, staff enjoyed their own coffee in the back instead of tapping into the shop's customer supply.

"Hey," Ron greeted halfway through opening the office door.

Patsy started and almost spilled her coffee. She twirled around in the chair, taking in his chestnut eyes, and salt-and-pepper short-cut hair above a brief gray beard.

"Sorry. Did I scare you?" Ron asked gently.

Patsy shook her head. "Not at all. How is it out there?"

"Good. It's really good." He pulled a cabaret chair from under the side table and sat across from Patsy. "You wanted to ask me something?"

Patsy's strong, yet sensitive hazel eyes caught his for a silent moment. Then, her stomach fluttered. *Stop it, Patsy. This is your boss,* she reminded herself.

"Oh, yes." She lifted her recipe book. "I have some ideas to help us get through that dreaded winter slump after the holidays."

"I'm all ears." Ron leaned in.

Patsy smiled shyly. "I haven't told you this before, but I'm a baker."

"What?" Ron's eyes lit up.

With a chuckle, Patsy opened up her journal. "I've only baked at home, and I used to give stuff away to neighbors, but I'd like to contribute to Java Hut. Only if you're interested, of course."

Ron spread out his arms. "Are you kidding me? Yes! Not only do I have a top-notch manager, but now I'll have an on-site baker!"

Turning the pages, Patsy beamed. "Well, wait for it." She stopped mid-way through the journal. "Okay…I have three new muffin recipes to run by you."

"Hit me." Ron placed his hands on his knees.

Patsy inhaled deeply. She hadn't shared her recipes with anyone before, and it thrilled her. "Okay…first one—spiced vanilla muffins with sugar crystals on top called Winter Frost. Second—spiced coffee muffins called Wake Me Up Winter Muffins. Third—Chocolate and cinnamon muffins with blue buttercream frosting, and a small sugar surfboard on top called Winter Mavericks Muffins." She looked down at the page. "Actually, the last one is a cupcake."

Patsy raised her head and found Ron's mouth gaping open. Speech tried to spill out.

Finally, Ron blinked a few times. "Those sound delicious! It's exactly what this place needs, and I hereby give you carte blanche to bake away!"

"Thank you!" Patsy shot up out of her chair, just as Ron did the same.

They met in the middle as Ron wrapped his arms around Patsy, and their lips accidentally met.

Pulling back from each other in surprise, they waited in limbo for the next person to speak.

Instead, a loud crash of plates hitting the floor shocked them into alertness.

"Uh, oh." Patsy's eyes widened.

"Let's go help them out," Ron mumbled in haste.

"Yes, let's." She snatched her journal off the floor where it landed and tossed it onto the desk.

They marched out the door and onto the main floor.

****

Vivien hurried to grab a table for herself, Josh, and Brian.

"Oh, I'm sorry!" Vivien declared after yanking a wooden chair just vacated so hard it banged onto the floor.

The elderly gentleman who'd risen from the café chair adjusted his red plaid scarf and sent her a scowl.

Vivien's lips curled up to create the sweetest smile she could muster. "Merry Christmas."

After a moment, the man snickered with a grin and walked toward the exit. "Merry Christmas to you."

Setting the chair right, Vivien pulled it against a small round table.

"Here you go." Patsy set down a hot paper cup of peppermint mocha.

Vivien cocked her head. "How did you know?"

Setting her brown tray against her hip, Patsy's lips twitched. "Ron saw you outside and made it himself."

"Well, thank him for me, will you?"

"I will." Patsy rushed to another table.

Vivien watched her and tapped into Patsy's energy. Ron's new manager revitalized the place. Images of a five-year-old girl with short dark hair and hazel eyes in a little white dress filled Vivien's mind. The toddler played in a park on the Lower East Side in New York City. Vivien smiled. Now she understood where Patsy's slight accent originated. Once the little girl fizzled away, another picture entered Vivien's psyche. A fairly young woman in a 1920's black and white photo posed with a strong, warm smile. It had to be Patsy's grandmother, who hailed from Ireland. Patsy possessed the same solid Irish work ethic, and Ron really lucked out in hiring her.

Vivien got back to minding her own business and took a sip of her hot drink. Creamy rich chocolate slid like velvet down her throat, followed by sweet snappy peppermint tingling on her tongue. Vivien's eyes closed. If only today could be as comforting as her holiday coffee.

Coming back to reality, Vivien opened her eyes and gazed about. Sadly, she still saw her dead friend Matt in her mind's eye walking around the coffee house like he still owned the place. Even though Ron spent many a day and night on the premises, he knew nothing about running a coffee shop. Vivien surmised Matt bequeathed Java Hut to Ron as a challenge.

Matt used to say, "A man has to have something that wakes him up in the morning." Java Hut now did that for Ron every day.

"How is it?" Patsy eyed her cup after returning to Vivien's table.

Vivien leaned back with a giddy smile. "Miraculous."

Patsy laughed. "Good. Enjoy." She moved toward the front door to welcome new customers. "Hiya, kids!"

The senior citizen couple she addressed laughed with greetings just as warm. "Hi, Patsy!"

There was no point in dwelling on Krampus until Josh and Brian arrived. She might as well concentrate on what she still needed to do for Christmas. After fetching a pen and pad from her purse, Vivien got busy jotting down a Christmas gift list in between sips.

Java Hut buzzed with conversations from locals and visitors for the holidays. Peggy Lee sung *I Like a Sleigh Ride* through speakers, which made Vivien exhale a pleasant sigh. Besides an aroma of peppermint, chocolate, and gingerbread spice muffins wafting around the small coffee house, her eyes fell upon a collection of seasonal cards made by Half Moon Bay's elementary school kids. Usually, the left wall held gallery art, but for December, visions of Santa Claus, Rudolph, and snowmen covered the space. Joyous energy from the children's creations vibrated out to all. Vivien felt it, and she knew everyone who entered caught the vibe as well.

On the opposite wall, known surfers from their local and internationally renowned Mavericks competition covered the walls: Peter Mel, Ken "Skindog" Collins, and Grant "Twiggy" Baker. Vivien then spied a new photo of Ron catching a huge wave with confidence. Some shots portrayed Matt in his heyday, but the rest displayed surfing stars from all over the world. Their smiles were infectious. She believed that was why so many people loved the establishment, and of course the outstanding coffee.

To fully celebrate the season, shiny Mylar red and green garlands cascaded around the artwork. The adornment also spread across the bakery display counter and circled the front window. But the final piece of décor held the most delight for Vivien. In the back corner stood a full-sized Christmas tree adorned with small porcelain cappuccino mugs and surfboards. Some of the boards held little plastic surfers in different positions. When she first laid eyes on Ron's tree, she couldn't help but laugh. She'd never seen a tree like it before. On her last visit Ron told her his assistant manager Mary added red velvet bows and little white lights, which brought traditional beauty to its fun ornaments.

Vivien got back to writing out her Christmas list while waiting for Josh and Brian to arrive so that they could strategize. How odd that things could seem so normal while out there somewhere Krampus's spirit lurked, and was it only yesterday that she had defeated Dagda and banished his minions? The Java Hut seemed so festive, and it made it easy to concentrate on the gifts she had yet to purchase.

Donna and Roger: Wine tasting book

Katherine: Elf fuzzy socks

At the sound of wood scraping against the hard wood floor, Vivien raised her head and laid down her pen.

"Hi." Josh greeted her with a frown as he sat down.

Brian took a seat in the third chair and nodded.

They must have peeled out of their wetsuits fast, because she'd walked in ten minutes ago and they faced her in jeans, fleece tops, and flip-flops. She swept them both with a compassionate gaze, then focused on Josh. "How are you holding up?"

Josh shook his head and looked down at his wringing hands. "I'm freaked out."

Brian laid a hand on his friend's back.

"Look at me." Vivien implored.

Meeting her gaze with hopeful blue eyes, Josh held his breath.

She set her hand upon his. "I won't let Krampus take you anywhere. I have help in this department, and we can outwit him. He's ferocious and powerful, but he is also very simple minded."

Josh blinked a few times and began to breathe again.

"Hey!" Ron came over to the table staring Josh down in a friendly manner. "You're late."

Vivien stood. "It's because of me, Ron."

In curiosity, Ron looked from Josh to Vivien. He scrubbed his short gray beard with one hand, crossed his arms over his midsection, and angled his head. "Really?"

"Yes." Vivien crooked her finger urging Ron to come closer, then whispered into his ear. "A very bad demon is after Josh, and it's all a mistake. The monster thinks he did something against him, but he didn't. I have to protect Josh until the sun goes down today, or we will never see him again."

When Ron pulled his face away from hers, his brown eyes bugged out in alarm. He swallowed and lowered his arms. "Um…Josh, you take the day off. I'll call Cheryl in to cover."

"Thanks, Ron," Josh choked out, trying not to cry.

Leaning over the table, Ron gazed into Josh's eyes with intensity. "You have nothing to worry about. Vivien will take care of this thing. Got it?"

Josh managed a watery grin. "Yeah. Got it."

Ron gave Vivien a sharp nod and continued to another customer table.

Josh got closer. "Can I ask you a question?"

"Yes." Vivien sat down and moved in, as did Brian.

"When did Ron find out about the evil things you deal with?"

How could she answer his inquiry? Vivien told Ron months ago how his friend Matt really died. The demon Dagda killed Matt to torment Vivien, hoping to bend her to his will. Ron, being a bit psychic himself, knew Matt had not been accidentally electrocuted, as the police had concluded. When Ron pleaded with Vivien and vowed to keep the truth secret, she revealed the facts of Matt's death. Not wanting to scare the teens, Vivien gave them a partial answer.

"Ron has the gift of second sight himself. His sight is not as strong as mine, but he kept asking and wore me down. So I told him about the entities I banish."

Brian rested back upon the wooden chair, nodding. "Totally cool."

"Wow. No wonder he sees through my excuses when I'm five minutes late," Josh remarked with a frown.

Vivien reached for her peppermint mocha. "Yeah, just be up front with him at all times." She took a long sip.

Patsy arrived at their table and set a plastic cup of water down in front of Josh. "Ron asked me to bring you this."

Wrapping his fingers around the cup, Josh glanced at Patsy. "Thanks." He immediately drank.

Patsy smiled at Josh and moved on.

"Okay, let me explain what happened," Josh said, locking eyes with Vivien.

"You don't have to." She set her coffee down. "I saw the entire situation in a vision from the moment you pulled that Christmas fairy doll off the shelf."

"Oh…Okay." Josh's face froze at full comprehension of Vivien's psychic power.

"What the hell is this?" a middle-aged man sporting a candy cane tie raged in a thundering voice. When he approached the counter, a hush fell. All eyes focused on the man carrying his terra cotta mug of cappuccino to the barista.

"Can I help you?" Mary asked.

"Look." The man pointed down.

"Jesus, Mary, and Joseph—and the ass!" Mary erupted after gazing into the mug.

Patsy peeked over Mary's shoulder. "Well said." She murmured after viewing the man's coffee. "I'm sorry sir. We will make you a new cappuccino, and whoever did this will be reprimanded."

"I hope so." The man harrumphed and walked back to his table.

With a flash of her hazel eyes and a hand raking through her shoulder length black hair, Patsy faced a small group of women behind the counter. Then she carefully crossed her arms. "Okay…I know my crew, so I know none of you did this."

"I agree." Mary nodded.

"Does someone have an angry ex-boyfriend in the mix out there?" Her head gestured to the crowd of patrons.

Vivien stood. "You two stay here. Something's wrong." She arrived at the counter and looked down. Where a heart should be in the white frothy foam of a cappuccino Vivien read the words, "You Suck!"

Krampus!

Goosebumps emerged along Vivien's arms. The specter of Krampus had to be close. Slowly she turned to take in the crowd.

"Oh, my God!"

A group of four girls in their early twenties surrounded by local shopping bags scrambled to stare into another mug of cappuccino.

The fourth girl, a lanky brunette, leaned over the table to gaze into the mosaic cup. "That's not very Christmassy, is it?"

The group busted out in high pitched laughter.

Vivien made a bee line to them.

"That is so inappropriate!" declared one of the girls.

"Excuse me," Vivien interjected. "May I see, please?"

A girl with long blonde hair moved back, unraveling her hunter green scarf. "Be my guest."

The offending froth mocked her with the words, "Hello Fuckface!"

When a prickling feeling ran up Vivien's spine, she looked up to find Ron leaning against the rear doorframe with arms folded and an evil grin. His eyes shone red.

"Ron!" Vivien ran toward him.

Immediately Ron darted to the back office.

"Excuse me!" Vivien desperately maneuvered through a long line of customers.

Her hand hit the office door, which Ron attempted to slam in her face. Vivien pushed hard, and wood slammed against the opposite wall. A framed photo of Ron and his three lifelong surf buddies, including Matt, fell with a crash.

They both gazed down to see shattered glass.

A sound like a giant chewing on rocks commenced when he spoke. "A friend you will no longer be when he finds his cherished photograph destroyed." He glared through Vivien with hooded crimson eyes. Then Ron growled.

"Krampus, get out of my friend—now!"

His mouth elongated unnaturally as snarling words tumbled out. "I will get the boy! He shall suffer for his deed!"

Vivien rushed Ron, pushing him against the wall. She had to halt his misshapen mouth before the demon broke her friend's jaw. Krampus did not care about the body he inhabited.

"You will not take Josh, and you will leave Ron's body alone!" Vivien pronounced.

Suddenly, her back slid down to the floor after hitting the opposite wall. Before Krampus threw her around like a rag doll, Vivien tucked, rolled, and jolted to a standing position.

"Your spirit Krampus is now inert. The form of my friend you shall not hurt. Till sundown for me you shall frozen be!"

Ron's pupils expanded just before he collapsed.

"What did you do to him?" Josh yelled from the doorway. He stood in front of Brian, who looked over Josh's shoulder with eyes like saucers.

"Close the door. Quick!" Vivien commanded.

After the door shut, Ron's body began to tremble.

Vivien caught his eyes. Anger raged within.

"I need to bind him as well." She grabbed a long stretch of red Mylar garland from a box in the corner and tossed it to Brian and Josh. "Help me tie up his arms."

"What?" Josh shot back.

Nonchalantly, she returned his flabbergasted gaze. "Krampus has possessed Ron's body."

His head snapped around to witness Ron's furious face and shaking body. "Holy shit!"

"It's going to be all right, Josh. Just follow my instructions. Wrap up his arms with the garland. I need something physical to bind him in addition to my Triad chant."

Josh handed Brian the end of the garland. "C'mon."

Vivien pulled Ron up to a standing position and nodded to the guys.

Brian gawked at Vivien. "Wow, you're really strong."

"Hurry up," Josh barked at Brian as he started wrapping Ron's arms with the festive garland.

Vivien extended her palms and inhaled a focused breath. The Triad chant flowed from her lips a second time.

As they tied the final knot that kept Ron's arms captive to his sides, Vivien's invocation drew to a close.

"Good," She crossed her arms with a huff. "That will hold him."

Ron's body calmed, and his eyes relaxed. The real Ron came back. His look of surprise hit Vivien full on.

She laid a hand on his shoulder. "Ron, you have been possessed by an entity." Vivien smiled. "But don't worry. I've got you."

His brown eyes blinked, and a whisper uttered from his lips, "Okay."

"I'm sorry, Ron. It's all my fault," Josh blurted out.

"What?" he asked in confusion.

Stepping between them, Vivien faced Josh. "There's no time for apologies now. We have to get him to my house. Go back to our table and grab my purse. Inside is the key to my blue hybrid SUV parked right outside the front door."

Brian stepped back, focused on the shiny red Christmas garland strapping Ron's arms, and threw up his hands. "Okay, that looks really weird! How are we going get him out of here like that?"

"Bring the car around. We'll take him out the back alley. Oh, and please grab my jacket. It's hanging on the chair."

"Got it!" Josh pivoted, jerked the door open, and nearly ran into Patsy.

"What have you done to him?" Patsy bellowed in horror, looking past Josh to Ron.

Everyone went still.

Vivien broke the silence. "Josh, go!"

Josh ran out.

Vivien held up her hands to stop Patsy from getting closer to Ron. "I can explain."

Slamming the door shut, Patsy set arms akimbo beneath hardened hazel eyes. "Fine. Explain."

Brian slapped his hand onto his forehead. "Oh, man."

At a loss for words, Vivien's mind raced. She respected Patsy but wasn't sure how open she was to the paranormal. "Well...you are aware I'm a psychic because everyone in town has that knowledge. But I'm also a spiritual healer. You know, like reiki and crystals." She turned back to Ron standing behind her wrapped up like a Christmas present. "Ron is suffering from a bad migraine, and I need to take him to my place to remove it. Then he can come back tonight and work till closing."

Patsy cocked her head. "Even if I did believe that, why are his arms wrapped in red tinsel?"

Damn it!

Brian piped up. "You're a really bad liar."

Vivien glared at him.

In a split-second Patsy closed the distance between her and Ron. "Ron, what's really wrong? Tell me."

Ron grinned like a high school kid about to have his first kiss. "Hi, Patsy."

Patsy smiled back. "Hi."

Brian and Vivien exchanged glances.

"All I can tell you is that I trust Vivien completely, and so can you. She's only trying to help me…um…heal," Ron said coolly.

Only seconds passed before a cell phone emerged from Patsy's jeans pocket. She tapped on the screen and handed it to Vivien. "Put your number and address in my phone. I'm coming over to help."

Vivien shook her head. "But it's nothing, really. It might not be a migraine, but it's in the migraine category—"

"Migraine, my ass!" Patsy declared.

Their eyes locked.

"I'm not going to talk you out of this, am I?"

Slowly, Patsy moved her head side to side.

Releasing an extremely long breath, Vivien took the cell out of Patsy's hand. "Okay, but whatever strange things you see or hear at my house must be kept confidential."

"Agreed." Patsy put her phone back after Vivien placed it in her palm.

The office door blasted open. "I've got your car parked in the alley, but we have to hurry. People speed through there all the time, and it's really tight." Josh tossed Vivien's black and white satchel to her so fast, it crashed into her stomach.

"Thank you." Her tiny voice came out after grasping the bag.

"Wait. Let me make sure the coast is clear." Patsy disappeared into the hall. Poking her head in the doorway, she nodded. "Okay, go. I'll put Mary in charge."

The sound of deep growling made Vivien turn around. Ron's face contorted with torment.

She pulled her car key out. "Josh, you and Brian open the rear door, and then get in and wait for me. We have to keep Ron in the very back. Got it?"

"Yeah." Josh snatched the key from her hand, and Brian followed him out.

"I'm still here," Krampus hissed out of Ron's gritted teeth with flashing red eyes.

Vivien grabbed her purse straps and clutched his arm. "Come along, Ron."

After a few deep breaths, Ron's eyes turned back to brown. He darted an angry glance at Vivien. "Jeez! I hate this guy!"

"Me too. C'mon." Vivien pulled Ron along with her out the back door.

A moment later, she peeled out of the alley.

Chapter Five

Neal poured water into a stand at the bottom of a ten-foot-high Douglas fir Christmas tree. He rose from a crouching position and shook stray needles from his green Pendleton shirt. Deeply inhaling the nostalgic aroma of pine filling the room, Neal nodded to himself. Now it felt like Christmas.

Happy with his selection, Neal took a seat upon a long white couch housing red and green throw pillows.

A whooshing sound from the front door took his attention.

"I'm back!" Vivien's raised voice came from down the hall. Seconds later, she stepped into the living room.

"Surprise!" Neal waved his arm toward the majestic tree with a big smile.

With a gasp, Vivien moved closer. "Oh, my God! When did you do this? It's so beautiful!" She ran to Neal and gave him a tight hug. "Thank you." Blinking back tears, Vivien pulled her head back to stare up at him. "It's the most gorgeous tree I've ever seen." Then, she wrapped her arms around his neck and planted a big kiss onto his face.

After the smooch, Neal exhaled long and deep. "Honey?"

"Yes."

"Why is Ron standing in the hallway tied up in red garlands?"

"Oh!" Vivien dislodged herself.

Grasping Ron's arm tightly, Vivien gazed at Neal. "I'm taking Ron to my library, and once he enters, that room is off limits. I'll explain after I get him settled."

Neal stared back in eerie silence.

Vivien turned Ron around, and they disappeared down the hall.

Josh and Brian crossed the threshold of the living room after loitering behind the wall.

"Hey, Josh."

Josh's voice cracked. "Hi, Neal." He swallowed. "This is my friend Brian."

"Hey." Brian greeted with eyes downcast.

Neal peered at Josh and seated himself on Vivien's long L-shaped couch. "Please come over here, Josh. I have some questions for you."

Pushing his hands into fleece pockets with a face of dread, Josh made a slow beeline to join Neal. "Yeah."

****

Once in her library, Vivien shut the door.

A high arched ceiling offset a floor of dark brown oak. A cranberry velvet couch and two overstuffed velvet chairs—one emerald green, and one deep purple, sat in front of an oak fireplace. Books filled built-in shelves, surrounding a beautiful bay window with a tapestry seat beneath. The last dramatic element lay in a pair of long red velvet curtains framing the window, displaying the Pacific Ocean beyond the cliffs.

"Wait here," said Vivien.

"Where else would I go?" Ron shifted his feet.

Vivien grabbed the large purple chair and moved it to face the window. "Sit."

Ron seated himself in front of a beautiful sunlit sky

and then stared Vivien down. "Is this so I can enjoy the view while a vicious demon lives inside me?"

"Yes." She leaned against the glass with sympathetic eyes. "I need to mention something. He might try to talk to you, so don't you listen to him. Remember, you are stronger."

Ron's head dropped.

"What do you want to ask me, Ron?"

His head flung upward, but he remained fixed on the window. "Don't get me wrong, I'm grateful. But don't you just exorcise these evil things out of people? Why does he need to be bound inside of me?"

Vivien crossed her arms and released a quick breath, mostly to give herself a second to think. She could tell Ron a version of the truth but, being a very direct person, he would not accept it. Vivien had to lay everything on the line.

"Krampus almost broke your jaw. He would have succeeded if I hadn't stopped him. He has no respect for your body, and if I do a banishing Triad chant right now, he would mess you up horribly before I finished."

"That's just great." A brow arched upward when Ron turned his face in her direction. "So, how long is this going to take?"

"He needs to return to his realm by sunset, so no later than that. I have his physical body taken care of at the beach, and he will have to return to it by then. Also, I haven't exorcised a possessed person before. Entities I banish have always been on the outside. It's my first time experiencing this scenario."

"I get it." Sharply, his gaze shifted back to the window.

Vivien picked up he felt more annoyed than afraid

of Krampus. That made her smile on the inside. "Hey."

Ron gazed at Vivien.

"We will get through this."

"We?"

"Yes. Neal and I are your caretakers until this ends. Now…can I get you anything?"

He sighed. "Water."

"Coming right up." She gave him a kind, yet cheeky grin. "Don't go anywhere."

Light laughter erupted from Ron's throat. "I wouldn't think of it."

Vivien closed her hand on the door handle.

Ron suddenly peeked around the overstuffed chair and back at her. "Hang on a minute! Who's handling everything at Java Hut?"

"Patsy and Mary."

He settled down again. "Thank God for them. At least I can set that fear aside."

Vivien slipped out the door.

****

Neal came striding toward Vivien.

"I know everything. At least, I know what Josh told me." He gently cradled Vivien's face in his hands. "Are you okay?"

Vivien held onto his wrists and closed her eyes for a few seconds. Just relaxing into Neal's soothing energy helped her focus. She had to remain strong but, in reality, combating Krampus gave her nerves a workout.

"No, I'm not okay. All I did was knock Krampus's body out until the sun goes down, allow my friend to be inhabited by a Christmas demon, and delay Josh's trip to hell."

Neal moved his hands to her shoulders. "If I've learned anything about you in these past six months, it's that you always find a solution."

Vivien picked a few stray pine needles off his sleeve. "Well, I am about to consult with a Celtic goddess for guidance, so that might help."

Neal turned and wrapped his arm around Vivien. "See, I'm not even shocked by that sentence. I think I've adjusted to your occupation swimmingly." He broke out his million-dollar smile.

Vivien laughed. Only Neal could make her chuckle at a time like this. "Thanks, honey."

Neal walked her down to the kitchen where the teens waited.

After smacking palms together, Vivien called out. "All right! Check in time! Here's the plan, so listen up."

Josh and Brian sat upon black high-top bar stools on the other side of her counter.

Vivien locked eyes with Neal. "Please drive Josh home so he can retrieve that Christmas fairy doll, take it back to the store, make sure the cashier scans it through their system, get a receipt, and bring it back here."

"Right," Neal answered with a glance at Josh.

Vivien moved closer to Brian. "I want to thank you, Brian. You've stood by your friend and haven't freaked out. But I'm sure your mom is wondering where you are and needs help prepping for Christmas. Neal can drop you off at home on his way to Josh's house."

She stepped over to the refrigerator. "Ron asked for a bottle of water. I almost forgot."

Neal met her halfway and took the bottle from her hand. "I'll take it to him."

43

In the next second, Brian held his phone up to Vivien's face. "Read my texts."

After perusing his cell, Vivien nodded with enthusiasm. "Wow! That's perfect, and it's actually true. Every year I donate canned goods and toys to our local Holiday Help group for lower income families. I'd planned on dropping off bags today. So texting your mother that you're helping out is very psychic of you, Brian."

Brian grinned ear to ear. "Neal told us about it." Then, he got serious. "I'm not leaving Josh until this is over."

Before Vivien could ask, Josh held up his phone. "Same thing here. My mom said I can help you with your charitable donation."

"Good, and you've explained the doll mishap?"

"Yeah, I told her not to wrap it, and luckily she hasn't."

Neal returned to the kitchen. "Helping a person drink water sure makes a mess!"

With a sympathetic smile to Neal, Vivien leaned against the tiled counter. "Besides getting Krampus out of Ron's body, our priority is to keep Josh in our sight at all times." She gave them a wispy smile. "As for me, I'm reaching out for help to find a way to banish Krampus."

Brian slipped off the stool and peered into the hallway. "You can put me to work now." He opened one of the cardboard boxes lined up along the wall and pulled out a strand of evergreen garland. "These are your decorations?"

Vivien got a spark of Christmas spirit when she joined Brian at the box.

"I've held onto these for years. My parents used to put them around the mantelpiece in my childhood home in New York City."

"That's nice." Brian smiled.

"There's thin wire in that box you can use to attach them. Also, make sure the plug pops out at the bottom of the banister. There's a hidden outlet right there." Vivien pointed to a spot under the stairs

She felt a hand on the back of her neck. Vivien turned and received a kiss from Neal. "We'll be back."

Snatching a key fob off the side table, Neal called out, "Let's go, Josh! The sooner we pay for that doll, the sooner this will all go away." He turned back at the front door. "We'll pick up pizza on our way back."

"Good idea!" Vivien replied. "Fighting monsters always gives me an appetite."

Chapter Six

Vivien stood in the center of her meditation room on the second floor. As her arms spread, she let out a slow breath. Vivien created summoning words for the Celtic goddess of the moon, Rhiannon, who also served as her spirit guide.

BANG

Vivien's eyes snapped open. "What the hell?"

Rhiannon stood before her. Flowing midnight black hair framed luminous blue eyes. Upon creamy skin, a gown of shimmering cobalt blue cascaded down her body.

"I didn't even summon you yet!" Vivien stood with arms akimbo.

"I am aware of that," the goddess came back with equal mirth. Then, she considered Vivien for a moment. "I entered your realm unbidden to warn you."

Even while Rhiannon's voice resonated in a rich and otherworldly calming tone, Vivien's body filled with dread. "Warn me?"

"The goddess Hel is looking for her son Krampus."

"No, no, no!" Vivien's mouth resembled a fish gasping for water. "How do you know this?"

Rhiannon coolly twirled a moonstone in her left hand and eyed its glow. "You have your mortal rumor mill, and we have ours."

Vivien tilted her head. "Really?"

"Only this is not a rumor." Rhiannon's sapphire eyes pulled Vivien in. "Listen carefully. You must project your past life's form when Hel penetrates this world. Boudicca, as a Celtic warrior queen, earned Hel's respect, even though she was human."

"Are you sure Hel doesn't like humans?" Vivien asked, a thread of hope lacing her voice.

Rhiannon glided closer. "The point is I bought you some time. Since Hel is goddess of the underworld, she is extremely busy, and I gave her a distraction from her search."

Vivien's breathing stopped. "What kind of distraction?"

Glowing blue eyes suddenly turned to ice. "You don't want to know."

A tremor moved through Vivien's body. "Okay."

Effervescent laughter flowed from Rhiannon's lips as her eyes sparkled like sapphire once again. "I didn't kill anyone, if that's what you're wondering. Trust your instincts, Vivien. They have never let you down. You've got until sundown before Hel finds you."

"Wait! How am I going to stop Krampus from taking Josh? I can show him the paid invoice, but my gut is telling me attaining Josh is now a vendetta for him. He already knows about the mistake in buying the doll and doesn't care."

Rhiannon swished dark silky hair as her mouth curved into a mischievous smile. "But his mother might."

Vivien wrapped her arms around her waist, shaking her head. "No. I know about Hel. If she goes against me, she'll strike me down where I stand, with or without Boudicca's image."

Dazzling light blinded Vivien's eyes as Rhiannon's shape retreated to the back of the room. "You will know what to do when the time comes."

"I hate it when you say that!"

Rhiannon dissipated with a wave of her beautiful hand.

****

Vivien walked from her meditation room down the hall and stopped before reaching the stairway. She gathered thoughts about what Rhiannon just shared. How could becoming a tattle tale to a demon's mama be her new strategy to save Josh? After shaking her head in amazement Vivien continued to the top of the stairs.

Once there, she beheld a beautiful sight. Holiday evergreen garlands twisted downward and covered the banister in sheer elegance. Vivien raced down each step faster than ever before.

"Thank you, Brian! The staircase looks gorgeous!" Hitting the bottom step, she glanced around, but saw no one.

Brian walked through her open front door and then ran toward Vivien. "Just wait!" He huddled underneath the hardwood stairs, inserted the plug, and popped back out. "There!"

Little white twinkling lights illuminated the green garlands.

Tears prickled Vivien's eyes. "It's like going back in time."

Brian's happy face transformed to one of guilt. "I'm sorry."

Placing a hand on his back, Vivien moved her head side to side. "Don't be. I love it. It's just that I haven't put these garlands up since my parents died twelve years ago." She gazed into Brian's eyes. "Believe me, these are tears of joy."

"Good." Brian blinked and grinned in relief.

"Ron!"

Vivien recognized Patsy's voice calling from her entryway.

"Oh, no! I forgot Patsy was coming." Vivien sprinted down the corridor.

"There you are." Patsy moved deliberately to Vivien.

"Hi, Patsy! Nice to see you." Vivien responded with manufactured eagerness.

Patsy took a moment to size up Vivien's tone with squinted eyes. Then, she smiled. "It's nice to see you too, Vivien. Now, I'd like to see Ron."

"Well…he's not quite himself right now."

Holding up her hand Patsy stopped Vivien from talking. "Save it. I want to see him."

It was futile fighting off Patsy, so Vivien turned with a toss of her right arm. "All right, then. Come with me!"

"You're a little late with your decorations, I have to say."

Vivien turned left into her open kitchen. "Yes, I've been a little busy." She gestured toward a row of four bar stools. "Take a seat."

After dropping a small brown purse onto the counter, Patsy sat. "Vivien?"

"Yes?" she answered while searching for something in her walk-in pantry.

"I'm only going to ask you one more time. Where is Ron?"

Sunlight created small rainbows upon the wall under her kitchen window as Vivien held up a four-inch-long white crystal hanging from a slim silver chain. "Merry Christmas, Patsy."

A shadow of confusion swept over her face when Patsy reached out for the necklace. "Uh…thank you. It's not what I usually wear, but it's very pretty."

"You wanted me to be truthful with you." Vivien pulled up the sleeves of her red sweater and crossed her arms. "Well, here's the truth. You must wear this crystal around your neck while visiting with Ron."

Without a word, Patsy placed her head through the long chain and let the crystal drop onto her chest. She adjusted the clasp behind her neck and peered down at the brilliant crystal sitting on a white T-shirt with the head of a red-nosed reindeer in the middle. "Okay, why do I need to wear this?"

Vivien inhaled long and deep and spilled out words in rapid fire on her exhale. "A demon's spirit is inside of Ron because I attacked the demon's body to save Josh from being harmed. Krampus's essence followed me to Java Hut and chose Ron to possess. The crystal has been charged with protective energy by me, and it will keep you safe while you are in Ron's presence."

Dead silence followed while Patsy stared.

Vivien waited for shock, or a combination of laughter and fear, but neither came.

Finally, Patsy spoke. "Anything else?"

"That's it?" Vivien scratched the back of her neck, suddenly feeling an itch. "You're not going to tell me I'm crazy, or to go to hell?"

Patsy set her elbows down on the counter. "My uncle was a priest at St. Timothy's on the Lower East

Side. He also performed exorcisms for the Catholic Church."

Vivien glanced off into empty space for a moment. "On your sixteenth birthday he gave you a special mother of pearl rosary set inside a silver box lined in blue velvet."

A flicker of surprise crossed Patsy's face, but only for a second. Then she smiled. "Mary was right."

Vivien nervously cleared her throat.

"She told me you're the one who talks to the fairies."

Vivien's lips twitched. "Well, not yet, but I wouldn't put it past me."

Patsy got off the stool and dropped her purse strap over her shoulder. "Anyway, suffice it to say, I'm not afraid of possession."

"Wait a second." Vivien grabbed two water bottles. "I think he'll want more water. Tell him pizza is on the way, and you are welcome to join us for lunch."

"Thank you. Oh, and thank you for the necklace. Can I keep it?"

"Yes, it really is your Christmas present." Vivien stepped in front of Patsy. "Follow me."

After Vivien opened the door, they glanced upon the back of an overstuffed chair facing the window. "Remember, he needs to stay tied up in that garland."

"Okay."

"Come find me if anything strange happens."

Patsy nodded and proceeded into the library closing the door behind her.

Chapter Seven

"Someone order pizza?" Neal's shout reverberated through the foyer.

Vivien bounded forward. "Oh, great! You're back. Put them on the kitchen counter."

"Look what I've got." Smiling as he pulled a slip of paper from his pocket, Neal held it in front of her face.

Vivien's eyes swiftly took in a store receipt for one Christmas fairy doll. "Yes!" She snatched the paper from him. "I'm putting this in my purse right now! I'm even going to put it in my inside zipper pocket so it won't get lost among my cosmetics and tissues."

Brian and Josh ran past them.

"Where are they going?" Vivien asked.

"There's more pizza in the car, and Caesar salad. I got six large pies."

Neal pulled her close and held tight.

Vivien filtered her fingers through his dark auburn hair with a smirk. "One pie for each person here, really? What were you thinking?"

The corner of Neal's mouth curved on a chuckle. "Obviously, you're not familiar with a teenage boy's appetite. Also, I was thinking we'd have extra food for tomorrow, since we're going to be busy cooking, shopping, baking, and decorating."

She tossed her head back with tinkling laughter.

"Good thinking, honey."

Neal kissed her tenderly and then tugged on her arm. "Come with me. I want to show you something."

When they got in front of the tree, he released Vivien's hand. "Shut your eyes."

Vivien closed her eyes tight.

Neal's strong, warm hands pulled hers up and opened them. Next, Vivien felt cool thin metal on her palms.

"Okay, open your eyes."

Her most cherished Santa Claus Victorian era ornament smiled back at Vivien the moment her eyes opened. Father Christmas dressed in a vintage red robe in white fur trim displayed a leather sack on his back filled with teddy bears and snowshoes. He also grasped a rustic wooden walking stick and held a joyful smile. Vivien's mother explained to her how these ornaments were made when she was a child. The collection originated in Italy. First the artisans made the ornament from blown glass, then covered it with sterling silver, and completed the adornment by hand painting all the faces and details.

Covering her mouth with one hand, Vivien held tight to the ornament with the other. Moist eyes met his. "This was my favorite. How did you know?"

Neal's hand cupped her cheek. "I'm your soulmate."

"That's right."

"I wanted you to be the first one to hang an ornament on our tree."

She nodded and looked upon the gorgeous Douglas fir. After spying a perfect spot, Vivien raised her arm and attached the hook onto a branch. "There." Stepping back, she spread out her arms. "Christmas has officially begun. Now, if only Krampus was as jolly and contained these gifts in his sack, all would be well."

****

Patsy took in a sharp breath and approached Ron where he sat in the cushy chair.

She settled onto the tapestry window seat in front of him and set her purse down. "Vivien told me everything about your situation."

Ron gazed out the window sullen and silent. Then he cleared his throat and sat up a bit. "I suppose Mary is covering the store?"

"Yes."

Awkward quiet expanded into something almost tangible.

What could she say to help him? Patsy never imagined she'd be in this strange scenario. As the lack of dialogue got worse, she suddenly remembered the two water bottles. "This is for you." Patsy unscrewed the lid. "Let me know when you want a drink and I'll help you."

Ron glanced down at the garlands tied tightly just above his elbows and back at Patsy. "Thank you." Then, he clumsily tried to flick his hair back.

A sweet smile curved the corners of Patsy's lips. "Let me." She pulled a comb out of her bag and gently styled his hair.

Ron closed his eyes while she attended his locks.

"There you go." Finished with her task, Patsy put her comb away and crossed her legs.

"Thanks." Ron shifted in his seat.

After an uncomfortably long pause, Patsy opened her own bottle. "Aren't you thirsty?" She took a quick sip.

"Yeah."

Patsy lifted Ron's bottle and carefully poured water into his open mouth. When he grunted, she stopped. After setting down his water Patsy replaced the lid.

Ron searched Patsy's face. "I'm sorry."

"For what?"

"For getting you involved in this. Vivien tells me it will be finished by sundown, but for now, I'm just chilling. At least he seems to have settled down at the moment." He nodded to her with a slight smile.

Patsy wrapped her arms around her stomach in laughter.

"What could be so funny at a time like this?" Ron asked.

After recovering with deep breaths and leaning back against the window, Patsy gazed at Ron. "You're acting like being possessed by a demon and being trapped in red Christmas garlands is normal."

Ron joined in her laughter. "You're right." Then, he considered her thoughtfully. "Have I told you how much you've helped me with re-launching Java Hut?"

Patsy leaned in. "Yes, Ron. Several times."

"Well, it bears repeating. These past four months you've taught me so much. When I saw you walk through the door for your interview and recognized you from the kid's clothing store down the street, I knew you were the perfect manager for the job."

"Thank you." Patsy peeked out the window at a beautiful sunlit day. "After Kids Place closed, I began an attempt at retirement. I know, fifty is early to retire, but I thought I'd take a rest."

"How did that go?"

She locked eyes with him. "I was bored stiff on day two."

They laughed heartily.

"So, that's when I heard you were taking over Matt's coffee house." Patsy flicked one hand in the air. "The rest is history."

With a glad smile, Ron nodded.

"Hey, I never asked if you're going to keep running HMB Surfs."

Ron set his head against the velvet back of the chair. "My son is so good at it I let him take the reins. He's thirty now, but even at twenty-five he had an emotional maturity and work ethic I didn't have at that age."

"Really?"

"Oh, yeah. When I was twenty-five all I wanted to do was surf. I got a communications degree in college and intended to do nothing with it. Then I started making surfboards, and people liked them."

"It's nice your son continues the family business."

Ron moved closer. "I've been meaning to confess something."

"Yes?"

"I've been asking about you." Ron's head popped up suddenly. "Not in a creepy way."

She chuckled. "I know that."

"I understand you've been divorced for a couple years now, but I wonder if you'd like to have dinner with me at Pasta Moon on New Year's Eve."

Patsy's breath caught for two seconds. Did she really just get asked out on a dinner date by the man she's attracted to on the best night ever—New Year's Eve?

Their eyes met for a moment, and then Patsy uttered her response. "I'd love to." She picked up the bottle and held it to his lips.

Ron let out a long whoosh of air. "Wonderful! I actually talked to the owner, who's a friend of mine and had him book us a reservation. I didn't know if you'd say yes, but they book up fast, and I wanted to have it covered." Ron shrugged. "You know what I mean." He took a gulp of water.

"Yes, I know what you mean. Good planning." Patsy picked up her water, almost dropping it on the floor. "Oops." She turned to Ron. "Now that you brought it up, I'm very sorry your wife passed away."

"Thank you."

"Even though it was five years ago, some people never quite get over something like that." Patsy nervously wiped her palms on her jeans.

Ron gazed at her. "I had a wonderful life with Janine. The pain of losing her was unbearable for many years. I threw myself into our surfboard company, worked obsessively, almost drove my son nuts, and now I'm finally happy again. I'm ready to move on."

They looked at each other as if for the first time.

Suddenly, Ron growled while his eyes narrowed and turned red. "I'm listening you pathetic, puny humans, and I shall get that naughty child!"

The door burst open, and Neal announced himself. "Lunch!" He made his way to the long, dark-wood coffee table in front of the couch and set down two plates. "I got you both two slices each and added some Caesar salad." He faced them with concern. "You two okay?"

Patsy peered at Ron with lifted brows. "Are we

okay?"

Ron's eyes returned to normal. He stood. "Yep, we're fine."

Patsy followed Ron. "Thanks so much."

Neal strode to the doorjamb. "Sure. Do you two want a soda?"

"No, we're good with water." Patsy answered as she sat next to Ron.

"All right. Just holler if you need anything." Neal left, shutting the door behind him.

Ron shook his head. "Usually, I dig into pizza in seconds, but this is going to be tricky."

After fetching a piping hot slice from Ron's plate, Patsy smirked. "Once again, allow me."

He chuckled as Patsy held out the slice for Ron to eat. "Okay, Krampus, now you're in for a treat."

After munching on delicious cheese and mushroom pizza, so thick the tomato sauce oozed out the sides each time they took a bite, Ron and Patsy relaxed into a long conversation.

Patsy laughed heartily as Ron shared another surfing wipeout story. His brown eyes glistened every time he glanced upon her.

"Well, I'll sit on the beach and watch you surf one day, but I'm not getting on a board myself."

A long, dark brow lifted as Ron considered her. "No?"

"No." Patsy's bright hazel eyes met his, her voice firm, yet embracing.

After a sizzling silence, Ron let out a loud belly laugh. "All right, you win! I'll surf. You swim."

With a shy smile, Patsy turned her body on the cozy couch to face him head on. "Now I have a question for you."

Ron eased back. "Yes?"

"Since my cousins are out of town this Christmas Eve, I'm on my own this year."

She noticed Ron's eyes brighten.

Patsy's tone dropped to almost a whisper. "Would you like to come over to my house and share a nice quiet Christmas Eve?"

"Yes…Yes, I would."

Ron's voice sounded casual, but excitement simmered underneath.

"That's wonderful." Patsy had been gripping the armrest and now let go.

Shaking his head from side to side, Ron's voice raised in volume. "I have a very serious condition that must be met, however."

Patsy crossed her arms. "Okay."

A big fat smile covered Ron's face. "You have to come to my son's house on Christmas day and open gifts with me and his family."

"That would be wonderful!" Patsy cried.

Suddenly Ron's body jerked away from her. "Enough!"

"Ron, are you okay?" Patsy lightly touched his shoulder.

Low guttural noises emitted from Ron's lips.

"Are you still hungry?"

"Get away from me, woman!" Red eyes flashed upon her.

Patsy carefully moved to the edge of the couch in a rigid stance. "Look, I don't know what you are, but leave Ron alone!"

Strange laughter emanated from Ron as his

crimson eyes peered into her. "You dare toy with me. I will hurt him if you defy me again, for I am—"

"I don't care who you are!" Patsy proclaimed. "You're dealing with Irish strength and Lower East Side grit, so I'm not afraid of you, and if you lay a finger on my friend, you'll regret it!"

Ron's features twisted as he lunged forward.

With only seconds at her will, Patsy frantically looked for something to fend off Ron in his altered state without really hurting him. A quick scan of the room yielded nothing, until she eyed the remains of their lunch. Reaching out, Patsy yanked up the last piece of hardening cold cheese pizza and smacked Ron across the face.

Drips of red tomato sauce and globs of cheese coagulated onto his cheek. Patsy once again glanced into the real Ron's eyes, which became sorrowful. Then, the fire came back into his pupils.

Like lightning, Patsy stomped across the coffee table and jumped off. She stopped at the library door and looked back one more time.

A strangely long sideways grin took over Ron's face. "I shall gain my freedom from this carcass—and soon."

Patsy's hands tumbled over themselves as she tried to open the door. Finally, the knob connected with her palm, and she pulled hard. With a loud slam reverberating behind her, Patsy breathlessly ran down the hall into the dining room.

Chapter Eight

Vivien worked like lightning packing her first gift bag. As she worked, her mind remained on Krampus and her predicament. She grabbed a mini-Santa Claus, hand painted nutcracker, three gingerbread scented soy candles, assorted nuts from Pastorino Farms, three red cinnamon scented bars of soap from Belle Farms, Santa taffy and peanut butter balls from Small Town Treats, white athletic socks, toothbrushes, toothpaste, small boxes of cereal, canned soup, and finally, a bag of tiny Christmas plush toys left over from Kids Place inventory.

Proudly Vivien gestured to her forest green canvas sack stenciled with a snowman face on the front. "Here is the sample of how each bag should be packed."

Brian peered inside while his index finger pointed to each gift. "Okay, got it."

BOOM!

A slamming door took their attention from the goodies lying about Vivien's dining room table.

Patsy whirled inside breathing fast and instantly molded herself to the side wall.

"What happened, Patsy?" Vivien asked calmly, so as not to upset her further.

Patsy's hand rested upon her chest. "Don't get me wrong, I wasn't scared. He just startled me."

"Did Krampus speak to you?" Vivien ventured.

"Is that its name? Yes, he spoke to me. He tried to frighten me, but I got away." Patsy grasped the crystal necklace. "I think this also helped."

Brian gulped. "What happened?"

Moving from the wall, Patsy placed both hands onto the back of a chair. "Ron shook his head from side to side really fast and then started growling. I think the Krampus thing didn't like our conversation. Anyway, his body lunged at me, which was all he could do with his arms tied up like that. I scrambled over the coffee table and got to the door."

"I'm so sorry. I never should have sent you in there."

"Oh, I'm fine." Patsy straightened with a strong voice. Then her lips turned up into a smile. "In fact, I have a dinner date for New Year's Eve."

Vivien beamed. It was time those two got together, but right now she needed answers. "That's wonderful, Patsy. But can you tell me everything he said to you. It's very important."

Patsy wrapped her arms around her waist in thought. "Well, after I slapped him across the face with the slice of pizza—"

Brian tried very hard not to laugh. "You did what?"

"When he lunged toward me on the couch, that was the only thing left on our plates, so I grabbed it and smacked him. I had to slow him down so I could get out."

Vivien scrubbed her face with her hands. "All right. Well, that's a new one." She turned to face Patsy. "After you got to the door, what did he say?"

"He said, 'I shall leave this carcass soon.' I'm paraphrasing a bit, but that's what he said."

Vivien pivoted. "That means Krampus could wake up early. What time is it?"

Brian pulled his phone from his jeans pocket. "Four o'clock."

"Oh, God. If the demon wakes up sooner than expected, he'll teleport over here and take Josh."

A vision of her meditation room snapped into Vivien's mind, complete with Josh protected in a circle of salt. "I can safeguard him in my meditation room upstairs."

Vivien sprinted into the hallway.

"Hang on! Where are you going?" Brian shouted.

"To check on Ron and make sure Krampus is still in there!"

Patsy called after her. "Get my purse on the windowsill, will you?"

"Okay!" Vivien yelled back.

Once Vivien reached the library door, she paused. Tuning into the room, she felt no danger at all. Her hand reached out, turned the doorknob. Slowly Vivien opened the door. Snoring sounds met her ears. Ron sat upon her cranberry velvet couch with his head propped back fast asleep and Krampus intact. They were both snoozing.

"Seriously?"

She tiptoed to the window seat and retrieved Patsy's purse. Then, quietly, she closed the door.

Patsy leaned out from the dining room doorframe with eyebrows raised. "Well?"

Vivien waved one arm upward. "The demon's still in him, and they're both sleeping!" She handed Patsy her bag.

Exhaling in relief, Patsy grabbed her purse strap.

"Thanks." Then she glanced at Brian. "Since I'm here, can I help you pack those charity bags?"

He pulled a new red sack from a large box. "Sure! I'll show you what goes in."

Patsy tucked her purse in the corner and moved to the other side of the dining table, which had become unrecognizable with the massive project they sought to accomplish.

"Josh?" Vivien called out, knowing he sat pulling tree lights out of boxes with Neal.

"You called me." Josh stood at the living room entrance.

"Yes." Vivien locked eyes with Josh. "I need you to sit in a circle of salt in case Krampus awakens early. Follow me."

Neal joined them. "You want white lights around the wooden banisters out front, right?"

"That would be great." Vivien gave Neal a quick peck on the lips.

"I need another slice of pizza first." Neal strode to the kitchen.

Once Vivien got Josh upstairs his nervousness slammed into Vivien like a rogue wave. She gazed upon Josh calmly. "No worries."

"I just didn't think you could save me with a food additive."

Vivien snorted with laughter. Even though Josh decreed himself a chilled-out surfer dude through and through, he also got straight As in school and came up with witty comments all the time.

"There's one thing I don't get," Josh continued. "How come I need protection when the garlands wrapping Ron's arms are keeping Krampus captive?"

With a shake of her head, Vivien walked across the bare hardwood floor to a pine armoire. She opened the doors and began searching for something.

A bit of sunlight streamed in from one small window adorned by white lace curtains.

"There's a possibility of Krampus shapeshifting while Ron sleeps. Since his host is not conscious, the demon can pop out for a few minutes. He can't keep it up for long, but if Krampus imitates someone you know and touches you, he can command your will." Vivien closed the armoire and peered at Josh. "We don't want that."

Neal suddenly burst into the room. "I don't know how you expect to cast a magic circle of salt when you left the container on the kitchen counter." With a sideways grin, he held out a cylinder of sea salt.

"Thank you." Vivien snatched the container. "I usually have a bottle up here, but I must have run out."

Josh moved next to Vivien. "Can't we just wake Ron up?"

"Let's just say it's not a natural sleep. The demon gave Ron a paranormal sleeping pill, so to speak. He will be fine, but a little groggy later. Unfortunately, I can't wake him from this kind of slumber. I didn't want anyone to worry, so this stays between the three of us, okay?"

"Okay." Josh nodded with a sigh.

A sound like a small steam engine commenced when Vivien shook the large vessel of salt. "Let's get started." Pointing to the center of the floor, Vivien popped open the salt container spout. "Sit there, Josh."

Josh obeyed and sat down cross legged on the floor.

Vivien fetched a bamboo wood folding chair with white canvas backing from the corner. She folded it out and placed it behind Josh.

"If you get tired of sitting cross legged, you can settle into that. It's very comfortable." Vivien gave Josh a small smile while circling him in a generous fountain of salt.

"Okay." Josh sat down in the contemplation chair.

Neal stepped back. "Aren't you doing a Triad chant?"

"Not this time. I already placed a Triad on Ron, so there is one in place. The circle will hold up."

Vivien closed the perimeter.

"All right, give me the rules," Josh remarked while studying the circle in curiosity.

"Don't break the circle. If you do, Krampus can get in." Vivien glanced at Neal. "Now that you're here, can you take the first watch?"

Neal's face contorted in surprise. "Take a watch? Isn't the circle enough?"

"Normally, I would say yes, if we were dealing with a pesky ghost, but this is Krampus we're talking about. I need eyes on Josh even with the circle."

"Are you joking? You know I have to finish the outside lights."

"Neal! I have to fill up thirty more charity bags today." Vivien threw her arm up in a dramatic gesture.

Crossing his arms slowly, Neal almost sneered. "Can't you get one of your friendly goddesses to watch him? Rhiannon or someone?"

"No! They are otherworldly beings. I can't just snap my fingers and have them do my bidding."

Neal stood scowling.

With arms akimbo, Vivien peered through him. "You know, I'm the one who saved the world yesterday. You said it yourself."

Neal got in Vivien's face. "It's not all about you—Miss—sorceress—save the world lady!"

"Hey, you guys." Josh interjected.

Vivien hurled the container of salt against the wall. Luckily, the spout did not open. She stepped toe to toe with Neal. "What did you call me?"

"You heard me." He did not waver.

Josh raised his hand. "Can I say something?"

"No!" They screamed in unison.

"You better take that back right now!"

"Never!"

"Um…there's a dark spot above me. I thought it was my imagination, but it's still there. Do you see that?" Josh's shivering finger pointed upward.

They raised their heads.

A black cloudy spot covered the center of the ceiling.

Vivien smacked a hand onto her forehead. "Duh! It's Krampus! He's trying to divide us so we will leave Josh unattended." She sent Neal a sidelong glance with a curl to her lips. "Would you like to join hands with a sorceress, save the world lady for a Triad chant?"

"I've never done that with you before, but I'm game." He shook out his body and then took her hands. "Sorry about the name calling, hon. I got a little crazy."

Vivien swiveled her head side to side. "It's all good. Now, let's power it up."

"A Christmas demon you may be, but never underestimate the power of we, for back to hell is the place for thee!"

Once the chant met Neal's ears, he joined in. Concentrated focus grew until a twirling dance of white light surged between them. A black, misty blob began bouncing around the walls to escape.

Pure light shone bright, until the dark spot flew out the door.

Neal let go of her hands and exhaled long and deep. "Wow, that felt great. What now?"

Vivien shrugged. "We still need someone to watch Josh." She retrieved the salt and placed it inside her armoire.

Two hands grasped Vivien by the shoulders from behind. "Honey, I'll stay with Josh. I can do the rest of the outdoor lights tomorrow. We still have two days before Christmas Eve."

Vivien turned and folded herself into Neal's arms. "Thank you. I'll come back as soon as the bags are done. Brian and Patsy are helping me. It won't take long." She leaned back and placed a hand on his cheek. "Just remember, if you see me or anyone else enter here and it feels off, don't let Josh out of that circle."

Neal's brows knitted. "But I'm not your level of psychic. I mean, I'm not psychic at all."

"That's not true," she remarked with a sweet wink.

Neal shook his head. "Yes, I know sometimes you and I can hear each other's thoughts, which still freaks me out, but how can I get rid of an evil doppelganger?"

Vivien closed her eyes and stilled herself. "You'll know how to draw from ancient energy when it happens." Her eyes fluttered open.

"What?" Neal's eyes rounded in amazement.

Pulling up the sleeves of her cranberry red sweater, she sighed. "Okay, I'm on a mission to complete these sacks of goodwill." Vivien marched past Neal to the door. "I'll pop back up soon."

"Hang on. What did you just say to me about ancient energy?"

With her hand on the doorknob, Vivien angled her head. "Huh? I don't know what you're talking about. I didn't say anything."

"Seriously?" He ventured with eyebrows lifted.

"Seriously." Vivien confirmed. "See you soon. I appreciate this." Vivien shut the door behind her.

Chapter Nine

Neal sat down outside the circle with legs crossed.

Josh's phone played a loud bit of guitar music.

He pulled his glance away from Neal to check his screen. Then, Josh's head came up. "I'm sorry."

"Why are you sorry?"

"My mom says it's rude to look at my phone when a visitor is in the room."

"Smart woman." Neal flashed a big smile.

Josh chuckled and turned his phone toward Neal. "Check it out."

A surfing video played on the small screen.

"Sweet ride, until you wiped out," Neal remarked after watching the full video.

Josh's head dropped down. He pocketed his cell phone. "I know. That's been my problem lately. I'm trying to qualify for the Mavericks competition. Usually, I do much better than that. I feel like I'm messing up my dream." Josh gazed at Neal, his blue eyes pale with worry. "I don't even have to win Mavericks or place; I just want to be in the competition."

Being a long-time surfer, Neal considered Josh's words. He remembered the same insecurities at his age and got an idea. "How does it feel?"

"What?"

"How does it feel to surf?"

Josh stood up. He grabbed the back of his neck with his hands, pacing the small area inside the circle in deep concentration. Finally, his pacing stopped.

"Okay, when I get a big wave, it feels like I'm flying. But it's more than that. When the air pushes back on my face and whirls around my body, it's as if I've left this planet—like I'm in another world. A magical world."

Neal studied his face. "And that is why you love it."

Josh spread out his arms and beamed. "That is why I love it!"

"I believe you'll be chosen to compete in Mavericks."

After flopping back into the yoga chair, Josh's grin covered his whole face. "You really think so?"

"Yes, I do," Neal replied.

"Thanks."

"When did you begin?"

"Surfing?"

"Yeah."

"It began with my dad and a dog."

Neal's eyebrows raised in curiosity.

Josh snickered. "When I was about six years old, my dad would surf every weekend. On his last couple of waves, my dad would put our black lab Sammy on the board with him." Josh continued. "So, one day I asked my dad if he could put me on his surfboard instead of Sammy. He did, and the rest is history. My dad taught me how to surf. But now he says I've surpassed him."

"Do you have a picture of this feat with your dog Sammy?"

After scrolling for a few minutes, he turned his device to Neal. "There."

"Your dog is smiling."

"Yes!" Josh's head bobbed up and down. "That's what everyone said. I think he was smiling, because that dog loved to surf! My dad even got teased by his buddies who told him Sammy was a better surfer than him."

They laughed heartily.

"Was it the same for you? Did your father teach you to surf?" Josh tossed out the question as he pocketed his cell phone.

Neal pulled his legs up and leaned against the wall behind him. "No, I taught myself to surf. My friends and I would give each other advice, you know, the pros and cons of surfing."

"Oh."

He inhaled and let out a long breath. "My father was a banker at a very high level and almost worked himself to death. My sister and I rarely saw him, except on Sundays."

"That sucks." Josh said.

"Yeah, so besides studying architecture from a young age, surfing was my joy. I wasn't good enough to pursue Mavericks like you, but I loved it. I still do."

Tilting his head, Josh focused on Neal. "Can I ask you a question?"

"Sure."

"How is your father now? I mean, do you see him?"

Neal gave a quick nod. "Yes, I visit my parents in Palm Springs each year. But it took me a long time to forgive him. After his heart attack he lightened up. He even retired early at fifty-eight."

Josh raked blond hair out of his eyes that had fallen askew. "Wow, that is early from what my dad says. I'm glad he took it seriously."

Neal sat stone faced. "Yes, and immediately he asked to spend time with me. But his sudden turn around made me even more angry."

"How long did it take you?" Josh asked in a soft voice.

Neal grasped his knees. "For a year I didn't speak to him. My mom and sister tried to sway me, but I wasn't having it. Then, my friend George called. His father crashed his pickup truck on Highway 1 and died instantly." He clasped his hands together and gazed down. "George cried on the phone with me. He didn't even care. His tears just flowed. My friend told me to cherish my father being alive and forgive him. Then he hung up."

Silence suspended the air between them.

"That was amazing."

"Yes, it was. He's a good friend." Neal stood and walked to the window. "I got up the courage to meet with my dad. When I did, I screamed at him. I told him exactly what I thought about my first thirty years of not having him in my life. One day a week didn't even cut it." He put his hands in his pants pockets and took another breath. "Jeez, I haven't thought about this for so long. I haven't even told Vivien about that time in my life."

"Really?" Josh perked up in surprise.

Neal smiled on a huff of exhaling air. "Yeah, I will eventually."

"So, what did your father do after you yelled at

him?"

"He understood. Very calmly and quietly, my dad understood. Then we both cried and hugged each other." Neal turned back to the window again. "That was ten years ago."

BAM, BAM, BAM!

Neal and Josh's heads darted toward the door at the sound of three hard knocks.

"Josh, are you okay? It's Brian."

Neal moved to the edge of the circle in a flash. "Invite him in. I have a feeling he's not going away. But I'm telling you right now, that is not your friend."

Get Vivien's sword.

That thought blasted into Neal's mind like a lightning bolt. It didn't surprise him, because little did Vivien know, Neal practiced with his own sword up until their battle yesterday. Once he came to terms with his Roman Empire past life, he found great satisfaction in swordplay and even hired a coach.

Quickly, he flicked open the armoire and gripped the hilt of a long Celtic blade. Neal placed an index finder over his mouth, then moved into a shadowed corner.

Josh's eyes got big as he slowly nodded.

"Hey, Brian! Yeah, come in." Josh's voice broke a bit as he stood up.

The door opened, and Brian stepped inside. "Dude, I was worried about you." He looked down and back at Josh. "What is that? Salt?"

Laughing as best he could, Josh threw up his arms. "Yeah. Vivien seems to think it keeps out demons and stuff."

"That's totally insane." Brian shook his head.

Neal knew something wasn't right. Brian avoided direct eye contact with Josh.

"Vivien and her friend are finishing donation bags, so I'm putting lights on the Christmas tree. The tree looks rad, but I can't cover the bottom by myself. Can you help me out?" Brian gestured to the door.

"I have to stay here." Josh murmured.

Brian's human gestures became very strange. It was as if he didn't know what to do with his hands or arms.

"Vivien's down there, so you'll be safe. Let's go!" Brian reached over the salt line to take Josh by the hand.

Josh moved back. "No."

"C'mon, bro! It's Christmas!" Brian persisted.

Stepping back farther, Josh vehemently shook his head from side to side.

Suddenly, Brian disappeared.

Josh turned around to find Brian behind him.

"Oh, shit!" Neal gasped in a tight whisper. He needed to act before the situation got worse.

Then, Brian smiled a bit too wide, with a bit too many teeth.

Looking down, Neal discovered Josh's right foot halfway over the line.

Brian reached out with his mouth grotesquely open exposing razor-sharp teeth.

Neal closed his eyes tight. *What can I do against this demon? I don't know what to do.* Anxiety grew inside his chest, until Neal had no choice but to release his angst. For, if he did not, Josh would suffer. Grasping the hilt of the blade he remembered Gaius in battle—fearless, confident, focused, and triumphant.

Neal charged from the shadows with his Celtic blade hoisted and a battle cry.

"*Invictus*!"

After a deafening growl, Brian's body evaporated into particles and disappeared.

Silence.

Neal sat on the floor fixing the break in the salt line.

Josh lay for a moment on his back. Slowly he raised himself up on one elbow.

"Like I said, that wasn't Brian." Neal smiled and returned the sword to its resting place inside the armoire.

"So that was…"

"That was a Krampus manifestation."

Josh sat upright. "It looked just like him."

"That's what demons do."

Josh ran his fingers through his hair. "Thanks."

"You're welcome."

After a gap, Josh spoke. "Hey, what does *invictus* mean?"

"It means unconquered. Roman generals and soldiers used it in ancient times as their battle cry. It just popped into my head."

"So, is that why you yelled it out?"

Neal shook his head. "I think so. A lot has happened to me in the past six months that I can't explain, but it's all good."

"You looked pretty cool with that sword!"

Neal chuckled.

Vivien ran over the threshold. "Is everyone all right? I heard that horrible growl."

"Yep, we're fine." Neal stepped toward her. "I

don't think he'll try that again, do you?"

Glancing from Josh to Neal, she let out a breath. "Nope. I think the show is over for this afternoon. Josh, you're free to go downstairs."

Josh zoomed out the door in under three seconds.

Neal glanced from Josh's backside to find Vivien smiling upon him.

"Whatever you did worked."

"Well…I'm not ready to explain it to you, but I will soon."

With hands on hips, Vivien cocked her head. "We are becoming quite the paranormal banishing couple."

Neal laughed hard, pulled Vivien close, and gave her a kiss. "Yes, we are."

****

Vivien rubbed her hands together and scanned the box of ornaments at her feet.

Brian and Josh just finished adorning the tree with white lights and took a break on the couch. They munched on a box of sugar cookies Vivien that picked up that morning. Vivien had taken a look in on Ron, and he was still fast asleep.

Grasping a train enclosed in glass, Vivien hung it upon a strong branch. The locomotive looked as if it traveled through the Swiss Alps and carried toys in open cars with a Christmas wreath above the headlamp. Once suspended in place, Vivien called Neal over. "Watch." She pushed a button on the bottom, and the train moved in a circle. Every time the engine came into sight a high-pitched sound emitted.

CHOO CHOO!

Neal drew her beside him with a big smile. "I love it." Then he tugged one of the cardboard boxes closer.

"Okay, we have a lot more to do. I got us a very big tree."

A short, muscular man sporting cropped black hair and matching moustache entered the room. "Great Christmas tree!"

Everyone in the room turned their heads around in unison.

The newcomer wore jeans, a white T-shirt, and an open navy-blue jacket with the logo Bay Foods embroidered on the chest.

"Rocky, what are you doing here?" Vivien asked.

Rocky balanced a piece of veggie pizza in one hand and handed her a paper printout with the other. "You submitted a grocery order online this morning with delivery after three o'clock this afternoon. Well…it's after three o'clock." He gave Vivien the paperwork and focused on the last half of his slice.

Vivien reviewed the order in her hands and realized she'd put it together yesterday after her battle victory celebration eased off but forgot to hit submit. She remembered when she had been gift shopping that morning. All her baking supplies, as well as fruits and vegetables had just been delivered.

"That's right! Thank you, Rocky. I need to sign for you."

"Here you go." He presented her with a pen and finished his pizza.

Vivien scrawled her name and ripped off the customer copy. "How come I didn't see you come in?" She handed him the signed receipt and pen.

"Your instructions said the back door to your kitchen would be open and to come in and drop off next to the pantry." Rocky stuffed the paper into his jacket pocket.

Vivien sighed. "Wow. I guess I'm suffering from short term memory loss."

Rocky laughed. "No problem, and thanks for the pizza."

"You're welcome. Who gave it to you?"

"Patsy."

"Of course, Merry Christmas!" Vivien dropped the sheet of paper onto her coffee table.

"Merry Christmas!" Rocky held up a hand and turned away. Then, he stopped and smirked back at them. "By the way, that was a wicked Christmas prank you pulled on Ron." He shook his head and chuckled. "I didn't think you had it in you."

A chill ran down Vivien's entire body, head to toe. She glanced at Neal, who stared back in alarm.

"What do you mean, Rocky?" Neal took two long strides closer to him.

Vivien followed Neal. They stood side by side.

Rocky's smile disappeared. "Nothing. All I mean is if you like tying up your friends in holiday decorations, that's great."

Vivien grabbed Rocky's shoulders. "Where is Ron?"

Rocky's body quivered. "I let him go! Sorry, I didn't think it was a big deal. He called out my name from that back room and told me you guys forgot about him. He said it was all a joke that went awry."

"Stay here with Josh!" Vivien yelled back at Neal as she dashed down the corridor.

Patsy popped her head out from the dining room. "What's happening?"

"I don't know, man. But these people are really

serious about their practical jokes," Rocky answered and exited swiftly out the back door.

After Vivien hurled her body into the library, she tried to catch her breath. The room stood empty. "Oh, God! Where is he?" Vivien searched under the couch and behind her desk.

Suddenly, movement outside on the back lawn caught her attention. Vivien crossed the room to glance out her bay window. Ron sat upon the grass swaying back and forth with his head in his hands.

Vivien ran outside to Ron and kneeled down. "Ron? Ron? It's me, Vivien. How do you feel?"

Glassy brown eyes stared back at Vivien. After a pause, Ron's mouth formed words. "My mouth is bone dry."

"Yes, dehydration is a symptom of possession."

"Wonderful." Ron frowned.

Framing his face with her palms, Vivien gazed into Ron's eyes and tuned into his mind. Krampus no longer inhabited his body. She figured as much by Ron's behavior but had to be sure.

Patsy emerged from her back door and rushed toward them.

"You're going to be okay, Ron. Patsy can get you an energy drink with electrolytes. I've got plenty in the fridge."

"Thank you."

"C'mon, Ron." Patsy helped Ron up. Then, she glanced at Vivien with a questioning look. "Is he still—"

"No, he is himself now," Vivien confirmed.

Patsy gave a sigh of relief, and they walked back to the house.

A refreshing breeze kicked up, and Vivien inhaled. Her chocolate brown hair flew back from her face and for just a moment, she peered out at a deep blue sea shimmering in the sunlight like little crystals.

Neal, followed by Josh and Brian, ran to Vivien.

"Is Ron all right?" Neal asked.

Vivien turned away from the picturesque ocean and faced Neal. "Yes, Ron will be fine. He just needs to hydrate."

Vivien crossed her arms over her head and breathed out. "I need a few minutes. I've got to track Krampus down. I believe he's already slipped into another body."

"What about him waking up early and going into his own body?" Neal asked with a knitted brow.

"Nope. Now I know he was trying to scare us. He will awaken after the sun goes down, just like I thought."

Neal stepped away. "Okay, honey, I'll let you do your psychic connection thing. I know you have to be alone, but give us details when you come back."

Throwing her arms down, she swiveled back to face the sea. "I will."

Vivien circled her neck around and shook out her hands. She allowed her mind to blend peacefully with the sparkling ocean and began her psychic search.

Faster than expected, Vivien envisioned herself walking up Main Street precisely at twilight. Her mouth curved into a grin because she walked right behind her neighbor Mrs. Anderson's Christmas caroling group. The singers paraded up the road dressed in Dickens era clothing. Short curls of fiery red hair, which Vivien knew to be dyed, shook as Mrs. Anderson bobbed her head about searching for their next song in her book. Her energy seemed boundless for a woman in her early seventies.

They reached A Chef's Delight. The popular cookware store also offered gourmet cooking classes and prided themselves on being one of Main Street's chief attractions.

Vivien's vision found her standing at the side of the carolers. They caught the attention of the shoppers and store staff, who came closer to the open front doors. Then, Mrs. Anderson raised her arm like an orchestra conductor and brought it down. Immediately *Frosty the Snowman* began ringing out through the voices of ten carolers. They sounded a lot better than Vivien anticipated.

Something dark suddenly pulled her awareness away from the singers. Stephanie, who managed the store, stood behind the front counter in a white and red striped apron over her white blouse and black slacks. Stephanie's silver hair done in a holiday style looked fabulous, but when Vivien settled on her normally blue eyes, they appeared red.

Damn it!

Stephanie, a classy sixty-year-old woman with tons of integrity just got possessed by a demon. Vivien purchased most of her kitchen utensils and pots from her and considered Stephanie a friend.

Why is it always my friends?

Now that she knew whom Krampus inhabited, she had to keep an eye on Stephanie.

Then Stephanie's expression changed to one of fury. Her arm raised and her index finger pointed toward the sidewalk.

Vivien shrouded herself behind the Dickens costumed carolers, and then Stephanie appeared confused.

Before Krampus could find her, Vivien pulled out of her dream-like state.

Once Vivien returned to the present moment, she turned the opposite direction and walked to the sidewalk outside her house. Vivien did not stop until she reached Mrs. Anderson's front door and knocked.

Her evening now included Christmas caroling.

****

Patsy reached for a thirty-two-ounce plastic bottle of a blue electrolyte drink from Vivien's fridge. Then, she plopped it down in front of Ron.

"Much appreciated." His eyes warmed as he poured the liquid into a glass of ice.

Patsy sat on the stool next to Ron. "Hopefully this one will do the trick."

He sniggered. "Yeah, I know." Ron took a long swallow and then met Patsy's glance. "I've never drunk two of these before, but Vivien did say dehydration was a side effect of…"

Awkward silence hung between them.

"It's all right." Patsy laid her palm on the white tile. "You don't have to talk about it."

Ron took her hand in his. "I'm so sorry about what I said to you. I'm remembering now. At first, I couldn't."

"There's no need to apologize."

"Yes, there is." His voice took on a serious tone.

Realizing she needed to allow Ron's apology, Patsy waited.

"All I can say is I'm happy you're in my life, and

I'd never push you away in anger."

Instead of commenting, Patsy squeezed his hand.

Ron dropped his head in thought. Then, his head jerked back up with a look of amazement. "Did you hit me in the face with a piece of pizza?"

Patsy let go of his hand, and her face went pale. "Um...yes."

After a slight pause, Ron busted out in loud laughter. "That's hysterical!"

Laughing herself, Patsy shook her head from side to side. "I didn't know what else to do. I didn't want to hurt you."

They guffawed even harder until breathing got back to normal.

Before their conversation continued, Neal singing *Rudolph the Red-Nosed Reindeer* floated down the hallway.

Ron and Patsy turned toward the living room.

"Now it's really starting to feel like Christmas." Ron stated as he picked up his glass and drank.

"Yes. That's one of my favorite songs."

When Ron set his empty glass down, he glanced at Patsy. "How about giving me a ride back to Java Hut? I feel much better, and I'm ready to get back to work."

Patsy's eyes brightened. "Sounds like a plan. Let's go." She gathered up her purse and slipped off the stool.

To her surprise, Ron took her by the hand, and they walked toward the front door.

They stopped at the archway opening of Vivien's living room.

"Thanks for your help, everyone! We're going back to work now, but come by later for a peppermint mocha on me!" Ron announced.

Vivien, who had returned from Mrs. Anderson's, emerged from the room amidst farewell greetings from the others. "How are you doing, Ron?"

Patsy jumped in. "He's doing great."

Ron pointed at Patsy. "What she said."

After a quick perusal, Vivien waved them off. "All right, then. We'll see you later."

Chapter Ten

Beneath the rim of her Nineteenth Century-style stiffened black bonnet, Vivien gazed upon streams of golden pink sunlight dipping low on the ocean's horizon. She didn't expect to confront another paranormal entity two days in a row, but hopefully, it would not turn into a battle.

The red satin ribbon under Vivien's neck itched like hell. She tugged at it again and again. *I wonder if this is how Louisa May Alcott felt when she had to wear a bonnet to market.*

"Let me." Neal offered. He gently grasped Vivien's flailing hands, placed them at her sides, and retied her red ribbon.

"Thanks." Vivien moved her head side to side. "That gives me enough room to move my head at least." Then she stepped back and took in the vision before her. Neal looked as if he belonged to the Dickens era. He stood poetically in a black dress coat which hung to mid-thigh, over black pants, straight white shirt, and a red holiday satin vest. The white high-necked ascot collar and black top hat completed the picture.

An appreciative flush took over Vivien's countenance. "You're very handsome, you know."

Neal tucked a few stray strands of hair into her bonnet. "You're not so bad yourself."

"Not so bad, huh?" She casually wacked him with her songbook.

"Ouch!" With a light chuckle, Neal extended his arm. "Okay, step back and let me look at you."

Vivien did as requested. She wore a kelly-green and black vertical day dress with a high collar and black petticoats underneath. Below her bonnet draped a long black cloak. She wanted to be as unnoticeable as possible, to blend in with the singers. The only reason she sported a red ribbon was due to lack of choices. Each bonnet possessed a flowing bright ribbon. But all in all she did not stick out, which accomplished her goal. The final touch lay with her half knitted black mittens. She refrained from putting on full mittens, as that would hinder her work for the evening. Her fingers stuck out and had freedom to grab whatever she needed.

"You are stunning." Neal touched her cheek. "But be careful tonight. Remember I'm here to back you up. And you're sure Krampus didn't catch on that you know he's at the store?"

"I'll remember, and I'm sure he couldn't pinpoint me earlier."

"Wait a minute. Where did you put the store receipt?"

Vivien opened her songbook. A small pocket had been fitted inside the black book cover. Mrs. Anderson claimed it kept tissues handy when carolers traversed snow laden streets. But since no snow fell in Half Moon Bay, she used it to place the precious white paper that would save Josh's life.

Neal smiled ear to ear. "Perfect. I have a feeling caroling will become a tradition with us for years to come." He took Vivien's hand in his.

"I have the same feeling. Let's go."

Josh and Brian waited for them with the caroling group.

They crossed Main Street Bridge to begin their journey along the most charming part of downtown's shops and eateries.

Far above their heads hung a wire banner reaching across Main Street made up of white lights sparkling like twinkle stars. Rows and rows of the glittering stars continued up the street every two hundred yards. Complementing each banner, black lamp posts stood wrapped in shining silver bulbs nestled inside evergreen garlands.

Mrs. Anderson's group of carolers, which now totaled fourteen, filled the sidewalk in front of Pasta Moon restaurant. Her original group consisted of families who looked like they'd jumped off the screen of *A Christmas Carol*. One seven-year-old boy even resembled Tiny Tim.

Waiters assembled at the front entrance, while diners watched through windows.

"*Buon Natale!*" Antonio, the owner, greeted them with outstretched arms after opening both glass doors wide. Above his entry was mounted a four-foot-long gigantic red bow, accented with strands of fairy lights cascading down the building on each side.

The chorus repeated his Italian greeting for Merry Christmas and plunged right into *Deck The Halls*.

"*Stupendo!*" Antonio led a round of applause from his staff and customers after their song concluded. Then, he orchestrated two of his waiters to hand out small white bags of amaretto cookies for each caroler.

"I'll hold your and Josh's bags." Neal whispered to

Vivien.

"Okay, thanks. Just don't eat them all."

Neal placed the bags in his pockets and sent her a lifted brow. "How can you say such a thing?"

Vivien laughed and then halted. She raised her head.

Sunlight dropped off the horizon like a lead balloon. Creepy tickling traversed up her spine. "Josh, come here."

Immediately the lanky teenager moved next to Vivien.

"Put your head down."

Josh grimaced. "My top hat will fall off if I do that."

"Okay, then pull your hat down as far as it will go," Vivien implored while continuing to search the sky.

Brian stayed by Josh's side and stifled a laugh after seeing his friend's hat brim so far down it almost covered his eyes.

"Shut up!" Josh mumbled.

"Sorry, dude. You look like you have no head!" Brian snickered again.

Josh stepped on Brian's toe.

"Ouch!"

Vivien came between them. "You two, stop it!"

The teens finally got serious, after teasing each other about their Dickens costumes for hours.

Neal rejoined Vivien after talking to Antonio. The owner recently hired Neal to do a new expansion to the back of his restaurant. "What's going on?"

"Krampus is about to wake up in his corporeal form. We have to get to A Chef's Delight right now!"

"Got it." Neal made a dash for Mrs. Anderson and whispered in her ear. Her face displayed confusion, but after Neal whispered further, the older woman glanced at Vivien and nodded. Mrs. Anderson understood her neighbor's mystical talents and did not question Neal's request.

With a raise of her arm, the singers followed Mrs. Anderson past Limestone Jewelers and the Half Moon Bay Hay & Feed store. Managers and owners of said establishments tried to wave them in, hollering "Hey! Stop!"

Neal led a choral chant of "We'll be back!" so as not to distress Mrs. Anderson's loyal listeners.

Upon piling up singers in front of A Chef's Delight, a strange sight greeted them. Stephanie leaned against the front door leering at the carolers with crimson eyes.

A collected gasp emitted from all.

Vivien slapped a hand upon her chest, where underneath the Nineteenth Century day dress lay a Celtic Trestle necklace. The quarter sized piece of silver was a gift from her mother on Vivien's sixteenth birthday to enhance her psychic gift. Swirling lines within a circle signified life eternal—never ending. Positive powerful energy emanating from her talisman always helped Vivien, and this night she aimed to protect her group.

Enclose us all. We shall not fall. Around us, I pronounce a wall!

Stephanie straightened and shook her head at the sight of their protection. "No!" She stomped her feet like a two-year-old. "No! No! No!" Anger turned to rage, until suddenly her eyes transformed from red to blue, and Stephanie's body fell to the floor of the shop.

"Somebody help her!" Vivien yelled out.

Two of the male carolers ran inside to aid Stephanie.

Mrs. Anderson pointed out to sea. "What is that?"

No one answered. No one wanted to answer.

A frightening fog took the form of claws and leapt over cliffs just above the shoreline. When it crossed Pacific Coast Highway cars squealed their brakes to a stop.

Glowing holiday lights emanating from Main Street storefronts eclipsed as thick black vapor crept up the sidewalks.

What little traffic inhabited the roadway ceased. It was as if nightfall folded in on itself. Car headlights flickered out, and the light humming of Christmas music pumped out of store speakers stopped playing.

Eerie stillness settled into Vivien's bones. Her eyes made out a dark cloud taking the shape of two large horns.

He's here.

Instinctively Vivien grabbed Josh's arm. "Don't move." Her heart ached to feel Josh trembling next to her in utter terror.

Neal insinuated himself on the other side of Josh to back Vivien up, gently moving Brian over.

Emerging from misty horns came real horns.

His filthy red robe followed until a leathery face, elongated mouth, dirty gray beard, and sunken eyes appeared. He stood ten feet high.

The stink of sulfur attacked everyone's nostrils.

As Krampus skulked forward, he pounded a thick redwood branch held as a walking stick into the pavement. His goat legs moved in and out of the partially open robe getting closer and closer to the cheerful collection of singers as he slammed the branch into the ground.

BANG! BANG!

Instead of her choral group and street onlookers running away, they gawked. They were not under the demon's spell, but natural human curiosity took over.

Before anyone could blink, little Tiny Tim marched up to Krampus.

"You stink!"

Chilling quiet commenced as the Christmas demon tilted his gigantic head to look down upon such a cheeky child. When his claw reached to grab the boy, Vivien ran out of the crowd, followed by the boy's mother.

"Stop!" Vivien commanded.

Krampus jerked up to glare upon Vivien.

Tiny Tim's mother screamed and scooped up her child.

Pointing a snake-like finger, Krampus bellowed and rattled rows of twinkle star banners above their heads. "Witch! You shall give me the boy who stole a Christmas Fairy doll, or I shall take all the children of this village with me!"

"You cannot do that!" Vivien thundered back. She held up the songbook. "I have proof the doll was paid for!" Bringing her hand down, Vivien opened the book.

Krampus stretched his mouth, and a colossal windstorm struck everyone in its path.

Suddenly, the songbook flew over Vivien's head. She turned quickly to see where it went. "Neal! Quick! Grab my book!"

Neal propelled himself after the book, but it was too late.

Krampus halted his creation of gale force winds and concentrated on a tall, thin boy under a long black top hat. "Ah…there he is."

His gigantic unnatural grin accompanied by those smoldering wicked words told Vivien Krampus would toss Josh into his hell bag and be gone within seconds.

Vivien pivoted in front of Krampus before he could get to Josh. Imagining her white light of protection around the carolers even more purified, she upgraded her vision to a golden umbrella of illumination.

Disgusting odor violated Vivien's senses when Krampus aggressively stepped into her space. He had to crouch down to actually meet her face to face, but crouch he did.

Vivien planted herself with feet in ballet second position, arms stretched out, and eyes tightly shut. Even her fingers spread out like a web.

Hot, dark pressure pushed upon Vivien with mighty force. Her body shook as she tried to hold back evil. Vivien hoped at any moment Neal would return with her book.

All at once, the heat pressing upon her stopped.

Vivien opened her eyes to find Krampus looking up Main Street eyeing Java Hut.

Ron and Patsy.

"No!" Vivien screamed.

The Christmas demon turned his disgusting head back to Vivien only to flash a twisted smirk and then strode up the street.

Chapter Eleven

"C'mon, he's going into Java Hut!" Vivien snatched the book from Neal.

Vivien picked up her petticoats with one hand, clung to her songbook with the other, and ran. "Josh, Brian, come with us! We have to stay together!" she called over her shoulder.

Neal held onto his top hat and ran alongside Vivien.

A group of four millennials whipped their heads around and started following Krampus, Vivien, and Neal.

"Wow! This show is dope!"

"Don't you know who that is?" The red-haired woman in their group pointed her finger. "That's Krampus! My cousin went to the Krampusnacht Festival in Austria last year. He's the opposite of Santa Claus. He's a Christmas demon who punishes naughty children!"

"Let's go!"

"Yeah, let's check it out!"

They crossed the street with hollers and laughter.

To her horror, Vivien glanced back to see a mass of individuals pacing behind them in the middle of the road. The caroling team, Christmas shoppers, and random folks holding coffee cups moved in to see what would happen.

Krampus's huge body darkened the doorway of Java Hut. Then, he crossed the threshold.

Vivien twisted around to address the growing audience before entering. "Go home, all of you! This is not a show! You're in danger! Mrs. Anderson, please get your carolers out of here!"

"But we're here to support you, dear!" Mrs. Anderson held up her songbook with a big, delighted smile. "We can even sing a song if it will help!"

At a loss for words, Vivien thrust her body back into her task and swiveled to rush into Java Hut. Her hard-framed bonnet smacked against the doorframe and knocked her to the ground.

"Damn it!"

Neal swiftly picked her up. "Are you all right?"

"Get this ridiculous bonnet off my head!"

Without speaking, Neal untied her jolly red ribbon with precision and haste.

"Thanks!"

Vivien raced up to Krampus, who had positioned himself in the center of the store glaring at all the humans inside.

Ron stood firm at the cash register protecting Patsy behind him.

Patrons exhibited more interest than fear. Customers seated at tables and people pressed against outside windows held their cell phones up. They chatted about how lucky they were to be part of an impromptu theatrical event.

Once again, Vivien held the black book high above her head, but decided to try a different strategy.

The demon scowled back at her.

"Krampus, I'm sorry for knocking you out earlier."

Vivien spoke in a calm voice. "I had to save my friend. It was simply a misunderstanding." She brought her arm down and pulled the little white receipt out of the book pocket. Holding the paper tightly between her fingers, Vivien dangled it in front of the demon's soulless eyes. "You see, he went back and paid for the toy."

Krampus lowered his head and deliberately read the words on the receipt. "I see." The monster leered, revealing corroded teeth.

Letting out a long breath, Vivien allowed herself to feel some relief.

Just then, the paper in her hand burst into flames.

Vivien yelped as she dropped the flaming receipt and then stomped on it with her Victorian laced-up black boots.

In disgust, Vivien slammed her songbook onto the floor and tore at the black cloth ribbon tied at her neck. She flung her cloak on top of the book. All that work to save Josh—gone!

Whispers of wonder spread among onlookers, fascinated by the scene unfolding in front of them.

Neal appeared at her side in a flash, eyeballing Krampus with grim caution.

Vivien slapped a forced smile on her face and crossed her arms. "So…are we good?" she asked in a cheerful voice.

The leer Krampus held transformed into an unnaturally long mouth. "No. We are not good."

In the next instant, a long funnel cloud rose from the floor beside the Christmas demon.

Everyone inside Java Hut covered their faces as napkins, coffee stirrers, and empty cups flew about in all directions.

After twenty seconds of windblown pandemonium, it stopped.

When Vivien pulled her disheveled bangs out of her eyes, her heart dropped to see Josh standing right next to Krampus. He'd lost his top hat and appeared disoriented.

Brian screamed from the front door. "Help him! Quick!"

Ignoring all dropped mouths of her audience, Vivien snatched Josh's arm and glared at Krampus. "You're not taking him!"

His magical black bag materialized, and Krampus grabbed Josh's other arm.

"Oh, God!" Josh screamed and began to cry.

Brian finally broke through the crowd. "Don't touch my friend!" He joined Vivien in holding Josh's arm.

Deep, rumbling laughter shook the coffee house when Krampus opened his dark bag wider. Then, intense growling filled the place as Josh began slipping inside a black vortex.

People observing screamed and giggled with amusement.

"This is Chris Angel shit, this is!" one onlooker yelled.

Neal clamped onto Josh, wrapping his arms around his torso to stop his descent.

Vivien shouted at Neal. "I proved it to him! Krampus shouldn't be taking him, and where is Hel?"

Struggling, Neal screamed back. "Call out to her!"

Amid Josh screaming, paranormal growling, and a jeering crowd, Vivien locked eyes with Krampus. "I'm going to tell your mother!"

Josh fell to the floor with a thump. For a moment, fear flashed in Krampus's eyes.

Neal and Brian helped Josh to a standing position and pushed him behind them.

Vivien faced down Krampus with arms akimbo intending to give him a lecture, but before she could speak another word, Patsy came charging up to them.

"Leave that boy alone!" Patsy shouted and splashed Krampus's face with a hot pot of coffee. Since she'd plucked the coffee carafe from the back office, Patsy didn't know Vivien now had the upper hand.

Utter silence permeated the space as piping hot black droplets ran down the monster's dirty gray beard. Even amateur movie makers with cell phones remained quiet, until someone laughed.

That's all it took. The whole place erupted in guffaws.

Krampus roared like an angry lion.

"Ron! Get Patsy out of here!" Vivien cried out.

Ron took Patsy's arm, and they ran out the back of the store.

Thunder broke out across the ceiling among silver clouds, filling the entire room.

People coughed and waved hands in front of their faces, trying to dissipate the strange fog.

Arising from silvery mist came the goddess Hel.

Hel's statuesque figure equaled Krampus's ten-foot height, but the mass inhale from all came in reaction to her face. Hel possessed classic movie star beauty with creamy skin upon high cheekbones and a lake-blue eye. Long snow-white hair flowed to her waist in thick silky strands above a long gown the color of cemetery dust.

But her glamour looks only covered one side of her face. The other side presented a dry skull. A bone hole took the place of where an eyeball should be, no skin covered her cheek, and Hel's dirty teeth stuck up from her jawbone. The rest of her body looked normal. In fact, except for a half skull face, she looked like a runway model.

Good God! thought Vivien.

She did not bargain for facing Hel with so many innocent bystanders around. The moment Krampus decided to enter Java Hut, everything changed. The crowd believed they observed a theatrical scene from the Krampus legacy, which came as a surprise event on Half Moon Bay's Main Street. But now the situation became dangerous, for anyone in Hel's presence entered a danger zone.

Krampus bowed his head to his mother, and she returned a small nod back.

All at once, Vivien spread her arms and tapped into her Celtic Queen Boudicca warrior energy to activate a ball of protection.

Before Vivien's golden light of defense could manifest, Hel swung her arm up and stopped her conjuring.

Like a movie freeze frame, all human motion stopped except for Hel and Vivien. Even Krampus stood inert. Vivien glanced up at the goddess of death while listening to the still piped in music of *Here Comes Santa Claus*.

Slowly Vivien lowered her arms and gulped. Even though innocent lives were now on pause, she worried what Hel had in store for her.

"Will you allow me to explain?" Vivien asked in a

surprisingly sweet voice.

Hel held up her palm.

Vivien stopped speaking.

Hel's single eye scanned to someone standing next to Vivien. When she spoke, Hel's voice came out like rich, dark earth found underneath all coffins.

"I've been watching you two all day long."

Vivien's head jerked around.

Neal remained awake and unfrozen. He smiled to appease the goddess and then pulled Vivien against him. "I have no idea what's going on," Neal whispered in her ear.

Not sure if she wanted an answer to her question, Vivien faced Hel. "You've been watching us?"

With a cock of her head, Hel cast an accusing eye. "Yes, and do you know what keeps running through my mind?"

Vivien and Neal remained silent, until they realized she waited for an answer. "No," they wheezed out in unison.

Hel crossed her arms and lifted a brow. "Why are Boudicca, warrior Queen of the Celts, and Gaius Marcus Antonius, Roman general, who between them are responsible for hundreds of my occupants in the underworld concerned for the life of one naughty boy?"

Vivien felt like she'd been doused with ice water. She angled her torso to glare into Neal's face.

After returning Hel's gaze with eyes of fearful shock, Neal focused on Vivien. "I was going to tell you. I swear, honey!"

Ripping her body apart from his, Vivien shouted a command. "Give me your hands right now!"

Neal thrust out his palms.

Vivien took them in a vise grip and closed her eyes.

****

Gaius drew Boudicca into his arms, caressing her cranberry red hair with the back of his hand.

"Come away with me."

"You already know I cannot. They would find us."

Silently, they stood within the old abandoned stable. A moonbeam poured through a crevice in the wood, creating a glowing pool of light.

"I must go." Boudicca yanked at her horse's reins.

"Boudicca, wait! There must be a way."

"No." She pushed open the heavy wooden door, gazing at the silvery meadow before her. "There was a time I wondered how my life would be had fate chosen a different path. If I wasn't in a position of leadership for my people, a life with a man like you may have been possible." Pulling the hood over her head, Boudicca mounted. Her voice caught when she peered into his cobalt blue eyes. "I thank you for your help, Gaius."

Faintly, a smile crossed her features. "I shall meet you on the battlefield." In a flash, she galloped away.

****

Vivien threw off Neal's hands. "I knew it!" She jerked an index finger at him. "I knew deep inside we were together centuries ago when I lived as Boudicca, and you never told me!"

"Now, wait a minute."

"No!" Vivien pushed hard on Neal's chest, and he flew across the room, knocking down a few frozen people.

Hel tapped her finger upon crossed arms with a

tiny smile. "This shall prove to be very interesting."

After recovering from being knocked on his ass, Neal belligerently got in Vivien's face. "Damn it! Listen to me!"

"Yes, Gaius." Vivien glared.

Neal closed his eyes, exhaled, and dialed his anger back. "Okay, remember when I brought over tiramisu and then we walked on the beach at sunset?"

Fire flashed in Vivien's eyes. "You knew then?"

"Hear me out. The next morning, I had a vivid dream before dawn from that time. That's when I knew I lived as Gaius and loved you."

Viciously, Vivien crossed her arms.

"But at the time you were in the middle of a battle, and your burden was to save our world." Neal took a step back to give her space. "So I decided not to add one more thing onto your plate." His eyes searched Vivien. "We have dealt with grief in this lifetime—you losing Philip, and me losing Darlene. So I made a decision."

A long moment passed as one human and one goddess scrutinized Neal, both with tightly crossed arms and faces of stone.

Finally, the human softened.

Vivien shifted her arms to wrap around her waist and blinked away tears. "When were you going to tell me?"

"Christmas morning. I planned on giving you a painting of Boudicca done by a local artist and speaking my truth underneath our Christmas tree."

Seconds ticked away.

Suddenly, Vivien threw herself at Neal's torso and tucked her head under his arm with open tears. "That's so beautiful!"

Neal sighed in absolute relief. "Am I forgiven?"

Vivien's head bobbed up and down against his body.

Even Hel appeared affected for a split second. She leaned her head to one side and made a sweet humming sound. Then she lengthened her body into a stoic stance. Stretching her arm, the gown fanned out like a storm cloud. Hel commanded Josh in a dark and sultry voice. "Come here, child." Josh woke from his frozen state and approached the goddess.

Vivien kept her eyes shut. Her heart glowed with renewed peace in finding centuries-old love. It all made sense to Vivien now. Neal seamlessly executed a Celtic blade on her day of combat and stopped her from stabbing him before she could control Boudicca's ancient energy. Of course, he battled as a Roman general centuries ago.

Suddenly, Neal shook Vivien by the shoulders. "Hey, look."

Amidst a fluttering of lashes, Vivien roused herself. What met her gaze jolted her.

Josh marched toward Hel in a choppy manner, as if walking through molasses. He tried to move his lips but could not.

"No!" Vivien catapulted from Neal and landed right in front of Hel.

Hel grabbed Josh by the back of the neck and revived Krampus's black bag of death, which opened in front of a large silver vortex.

A vision played in Vivien's mind with extreme clarity. Hel intended to wake Krampus and offer Josh to him as an example to Vivien not to interfere again. Josh would tumble down a black hole never to return.

Vivien had to be sharp, quick, and confident in the seconds that followed.

"How dare you as a mere mortal obstruct my son's work!" All elegance left Hel's manner.

"I would not have stopped Krampus if he hadn't made a terrible error!" Vivien bellowed back.

Hel looked down upon Vivien and seemed to grow even taller.

"Such an accusation is worthy of death," Hel proclaimed in a chilling whisper. With a wave of her hand Krampus awakened.

Krampus growled deeply and faced off against Vivien.

"Krampus dear, this mortal claims you made a mistake in attempting to take this naughty boy to our world. Is that true?" Hel angled her head and stared into Krampus's hooded black void of a face.

The demon grumbled for a second and then glanced upon his mother. "The boy is mine. I've made no mistake."

Hel thrust her arm out with Josh's body dangling at the end of it, as she handed her son his sack and Krampus opened his bag of doom wider.

"I have proof!" Vivien pronounced in a thundering voice.

Hel studied her with curiosity. "Hmmm…Boudicca's soul would not make such a statement if there were not some truth to behold."

"Behold this!" Vivien enclosed her fingers around Hel's wrist so fast, even the goddess didn't know what happened.

Hel leaned back and closed her eye as Vivien

shared a vision which began with Josh's purchase of the doll and concluded with their current moment in time.

Vivien hadn't counted on her life force draining away. When a human touches the goddess of death, their life automatically empties until they themselves are dead. Why didn't Rhiannon tell her? Why didn't she remember? Such knowledge was standard in 60 A.D., but her modern self didn't need to confront deities as often, hence the omission from her mind.

Although images flew through Hel's psyche with lightning speed, it still didn't take long to pull Vivien's essence from her body.

Peering at the tips of Vivien's fingers turning bluish gray, Neal panicked. "Oh, my God! What are you doing? Let go!" he begged, clutching Vivien's arm to dislodge it from Hel's power.

"I can't! If I let go, Hel won't see that Krampus destroyed evidence!" Vivien eked out through gritted teeth. Stinging coldness traveled up to her arms underneath the period day dress.

Suddenly, taking in air felt like inhaling icicles. Jagged pain entered Vivien's chest. She could no longer breathe.

"Stop it! You're killing her!" Neal shrieked at Hel so hard, his face turned red.

In the next moment, Vivien glanced upon twinkling white lights dripping from Java Hut's front awning, and then they fell sideways.

Chapter Twelve

Unknown hands tapped Vivien's face.

"Vivien? Vivien? Wake up!" An urgent man's voice murmured.

Suddenly, oxygen filled her lungs with a whoosh. Vivien's eyes popped open to see Neal.

"Thank God." Neal placed a palm on her cheek. "Your color is coming back."

Vivien found herself laid out on the Java Hut floor. Further scanning confirmed all patrons still stood frozen.

Neal helped Vivien up, and they embraced once she stood. "That was scary. She almost killed you."

Their caress abruptly ceased when Hel released a screech, which shook Vivien and Neal to the core.

After Hel released hold of his shirt, Josh ran to Vivien.

She grasped Josh's shoulders. "Are you okay?"

"Yeah," Josh answered in a shaky voice.

Hel drew Krampus to stand in front of her, sending him a wicked side eye. "Did you truly believe I would not see you set that piece of parchment aflame?"

Krampus's hooded head lowered. "I am sorry, Mother."

Vivien barely heard the low rumbling grunt which emitted from Krampus's throat. He had underestimated the power of his mother, and he knew it.

"You failed me! My own son! What passed between you and Boudicca was known to me in real time. She did not need to share her vision with me. I hoped you would tell me yourself, but you did not."

At that, Krampus kneeled in front of his mother. "I am at your mercy."

The goddess pivoted her body. "I shall speak with Boudicca!"

Vivien came forward and instinctively bowed her head in a quick movement.

"I apologize for the actions of my son. The accused boy is blameless of any wrongdoing and shall be released from punishment."

"Thank you," Vivien uttered softly.

Neal marched up to Hel. "You already knew what went down, and you didn't tell us! You almost killed her!" he blustered.

Hel casually waved her hand. "I would have revived her."

"Oh, that makes it all better!" Neal grunted sarcastically.

Vivien grasped his arm. "Honey, please."

Neal stepped back, shaking his head.

Waves of dirt flew off Hel's gown as she turned back to Krampus. Her arms raised in a very dramatic fashion. "Krampus you are hereby banished from any retrieval of naughty children on planet Earth!"

Krampus raised his large head with mouth agog.

"So shall it be!"

Krampus's magical black bag, still levitating, swallowed up its master and launched into a silver vortex. The Christmas demon's screams echoed faintly just before the wormhole closed.

Hel turned around with all the sophistication of a Park Avenue hostess. The goddess smoothed out her dirty gray-brown gown and then flicked her white hair back. "Now—you two." Hel peered upon the faces of Vivien and Neal and smiled sweetly. "I shall see you two later—much later." With a glint in Hel's eye, she looked up to the ceiling. "Who knows? Maybe you both will end up there."

Vivien didn't know what to say, so she just lifted her shoulders up and down.

Another dramatic swirl of Hel's gray-brown gossamer gown announced her departure.

Vivien lifted her arm. "Hel?"

Hel glanced back with exasperation, since Vivien halted her theatrical exit.

Pointing a finger across the still life crowd in and outside the coffee house, Vivien beseeched her. "Before you go, can you please unfreeze them?"

A low, dark laugh issued from Hel's throat. "I almost forgot." With a final wink she rotated, leaving a strong wind behind her.

Vivien pulled Neal, Josh, and Brian closer, pressing against the whirlwind. Vivien yelled over the airstream, "As soon as they wake up, take a bow."

Neal grinned. "That's perfect! It's as if we put on a performance, and now it's over."

"Yep!" hollered Vivien.

Like the flip of a switch, the mighty wind stopped, and sound picked up where it left off.

Scarfs dropped onto shoulders after being blown upward, but no one seemed to notice. Two people scrambled to a standing position from the floor, befuddled as to how they got there. Napkins, coffee stirrers, and sugar packets littered the shop.

A chorus of 'wow' resonated throughout the coffee house. Some people pivoted their heads around, a bit confused, but for the most part, patrons believed they witnessed the end of a show.

Vivien caught the eyes of Neal, Josh, and Brian. "Now. Take a bow."

Without hesitation, they formed a line and bowed.

Everyone applauded with amazed smiles.

Neal waved his top hat around flamboyantly. "Thank you everyone for coming to see Krampus at Christmas!"

"What?" Vivien muttered.

Neal snapped his hat back upon his head. "This has been a production of Krampus at Christmas. The cautionary tale of what happens when you provoke the Christmas demon who seeks to punish naughty children!"

Ooohs and aaahs mixed with laughter rippled through the crowd, ending with more loud applause.

Vivien chuckled. She knew Neal thought fast on his feet, but he really made the moment believable.

Audience members once again raised their cell phones, and cameras clicked off like wildfire.

Shoppers standing in front of Java Hut moved aside as Mrs. Anderson gathered her carolers together and led them through *Good King Wenceslas*.

Neal dusted off his top hat. "Shall we rejoin them?"

With a wistful smile, Vivien took him by the hand. Making sure Ron could hear her, she said, "No. After dealing with Hel and Krampus, I'd like a hot chocolate with whipped cream on top instead. Maybe Ron has some peppermint schnapps in his office he'd care to add?"

"Done!" Neal kissed her on the lips, and they got in line to place their order.

Once customers approached the coffee counter Mary got the staff back in full swing. Orders were taken, the floor cleaned up, and their huge espresso machine whizzed out hot, frothy steam.

Josh grabbed Vivien and Neal into a bear hug, and this time tears turned to laughter. "Thank you so much!"

"We would never let Krampus take you. After all, we need to see you win Mavericks!" Neal declared with a reassuring smile.

"Yeah!" Josh hollered and then draped his arm around Brian's shoulders. "Also, my dad never found out I drove his classic car! Thank God! I really would have been in trouble!"

Neal and Vivien stared at Josh in flabbergasted silence.

"You have to tell me what happened!" Brian pleaded with Josh. "Last I knew, that Krampus dude was after you. The next thing I know is that you are all taking a bow and Krampus is nowhere to be seen."

"It was pretty wild." Josh pulled his friend away from the crowd. "I gotta get home. Come with me. My mom will give you some pumpkin pie."

"Hey, you guys!" Vivien called after them.

They turned.

"Remember, this stays between us."

"Totally," the teens answered in stereo and walked out the front door onto Main Street.

Suddenly, Ron and Patsy rushed up to Vivien and

Neal.

"We heard people on the sidewalk praising your show." Ron snickered and crossed his arms over his chest. "If they only knew the truth."

Patsy leaned down and back up again. She handed Vivien a clump of black material with the stiff black bonnet and book resting on top. "Here is your cloak, songbook, and bonnet."

"Thanks." Vivien took the items and pointed directly at Patsy. "Remind me never to get out of line with this woman if she has food or beverage in her hand!"

Neal and Ron broke up into loud laughter.

Patsy put a hand to her face and shook her head. "I didn't know what else to do. That monster wasn't taking Josh on my watch!"

"Patsy, I was really frightened for you. But I have to say, seeing coffee dribbling off that demon's disgusting beard was priceless!" Neal cracked up and had to wipe his eyes for the tears flowing.

Guffaws started again.

Ron gestured behind them. "Let's sit down at the big round table." He pulled out chairs. "I've got something special I've been saving in the back."

Neal craned his neck to check the side counter. "Actually, I just ordered Vivien and me hot chocolates."

Ron waved his hand in a dismissive gesture. "I canceled your order."

"What?" Neal asked in surprise.

"You won't be sorry." Ron winked and turned to leave.

"I'll come with you." Patsy followed Ron to the

back office.

They pulled out tan wooden cabaret chairs and sat down.

Neal placed a hand on Vivien's back. "I think Ron is getting us something alcoholic. You need a drink, honey. It's not every night you face off against the goddess of death and her child-napping son."

"Ho, ho, ho!" a deep, throaty voice thundered.

Vivien's head darted up, and her body went rigid.

"Merry Christmas!" A large man in a full Santa Claus costume entered, complete with white fluffy beard and holding a red bag over his shoulder.

"It's okay. That's Wendell. He does this every season along Main Street," Neal assured her.

In perfect timing, Ron and Patsy came back with two Moet champagne bottles and champagne flutes.

"Santa!" Ron cheered. He approached the fake Santa Claus. "Welcome, Santa, to Java Hut!" Turning with his arms spread, Ron addressed the customers. "I think everyone here is on the nice list, so Santa will leave gifts at each table."

"Ho, ho, ho! I'd love to!" Wendell replied with a wink at Ron.

Spontaneous applause broke out as Santa placed small red boxes onto each table.

Having returned, Ron opened one of the champagne bottles alongside Patsy.

"These are left over from Matt's memorial last August, but I think this is the perfect time to partake. Matt would agree."

"He does," Vivien confirmed, sparkly eyed.

Shaking his head, Ron chortled. "I knew you would say that."

Vivien gazed at Neal with a blissful smile. "We did it. Josh is safe."

Draping his arm upon her shoulders, Neal whispered in her ear, "No, you did it."

"No." Vivien placed a kiss on Neal's lips. "We did it."

Vivien smoothed down her puffy Dickens dress with a relaxing exhale and looked around the coffee house.

This night she would never forget. Vivien cherished her friends, who had also become her family.

Chapter Thirteen

Christmas Eve finally arrived.

The bustling chaos from two days earlier no longer occupied Vivien's home. In fact, she and Neal planned a romantic Christmas Eve dinner. Vivien wore her favorite full-length cinnamon crushed velvet dress made in a 1940's style. Neal also went with a classic look, sporting a red turtleneck and black slacks.

Vivien anticipated friends arriving to enjoy hot mulled wine, hors d'oeuvres, and a gift exchange on Christmas Day with delight.

But for now, Vivien breathed in pumpkin pie. *Mmmm!* After putting on oven mitts, she clutched the long silver metal bar and pulled down. On the oven rack sat Vivien's beautiful orange pumpkin pie completely baked. Her timer dinged seconds before, and her nerves eased. The remainder of Christmas dinner was now complete.

Gently Vivien pulled out the pie and placed it atop her red ceramic plate. She looked up as Neal entered the kitchen holding a glass of merlot.

"That's it. We can officially start our holiday feast," Vivien announced while slipping off her oven mitts.

Neal picked up a wine glass already filled off the kitchen counter.

"Thank you." She grasped the stem.

"To us." Neal clicked Vivien's glass with his own.

"To us," Vivien echoed, feeling as if she melted in bliss from Neal's charming smile and dazzling green eyes.

They drank.

Taking her free hand, Neal led Vivien to the dining room. Vivien's lips parted with a swift breath. While she'd been puttering in the kitchen, Neal heaped two plates with ample helpings of cranberry stuffing, turkey, mashed potatoes, and green beans. Next to each plate sat a bowl of simple salad.

Neal waved one arm out in a grand gesture. "*Bon appétit!*"

"*Bon appétit!*" Vivien gave him kiss on the cheek and sat down in the chair Neal pulled out for her.

Rather than sit across from her, he sat alongside Vivien. Before them stood a four-pronged candelabra of long white tapers with plastic decorative holly berries strewn below. An enchanting aroma of apples and cinnamon wafted from two three-wick candles placed on the dining room hutch.

Vivien lifted her wine once again. "We finally made a Merry Christmas, didn't we?"

Neal clinked glasses with Vivien. "Yes, we did."

They sipped in unison.

With a lift of her fork, Vivien inhaled the delightful smells striking her senses at once.

"Greetings!"

Clinking of metal pounded in Vivien's ears. Her fork did somersaults upon the heavy wood table. When Vivien looked up, her heart pounded in panic.

"Hel?"

Hel stood before them in all her grandeur on the

other side of the dining table. Atop Hel's cemetery dust gown hung a blood-red hooded cloak.

A four-foot-high silver pewter staff emerged from underneath Hel's cloak. Encased in a swirling pewter claw, a crystal ball sat atop the staff.

"What is that for?" Vivien pointed, knowing the mystical rod had something to do with her.

Hel attempted to smile, which only succeeded in curling her beautiful lips on the flesh side. "I would speak with you, Boudicca."

"Vivien," she confirmed with a stern countenance.

Hel closed her eye for a moment and reopened it. "Vivien."

Neal tensed next to her, and Vivien placed her hand on top of his. "I know this may seem impertinent, but can it wait until the new year?"

"No, it cannot!" Hel demanded from right behind their chairs.

Vivien popped up on a yelp.

Neal rose brusquely.

Throwing up her hands, Vivien faced her. "Look, we're just trying to have a nice quiet Christmas Eve."

The goddess looked down upon her crystal, which awakened with swirling silver lights. She brought her face up to gaze upon Neal and Vivien. "I truly am sorry to interrupt."

"Really?" Vivien uttered dripping with sarcasm and crossed her arms. Where was her moxie coming from? Did she forget she faced the ruler of death? Now all she could do was await punishment.

But no punishment came. Hel stepped back and leaned upon her staff. "I promise both of you, our discussion will only fill five minutes of your precious time."

Two seconds ticked by.

"All right." Vivien responded. "Go ahead."

Slowly and deliberately, Hel shook her head. "Our conversation cannot take place here. You must accompany me to my home."

"No!" Neal moved directly in front of Hel. "You will not take Vivien to your home, because it is not a home. It is hell!"

Hel looked upon Neal with sympathy instead of anger. "Gaius, really?"

"Neal Harrington! My name is Neal Harrington. Will you live in the present for fuck's sake!"

At that, Vivien jumped in front of Neal. "It's okay! I'll come with you."

Hel glared at Neal with an eye of sinister venom, but he held his ground. "You ignorant human being! Five minutes in this upper world is one hour in the underworld. By the time you've finished your pathetic glass of wine, she shall be back by your side."

Vivien swiveled and looked imploringly upon Neal. She placed a hand on his cheek. "Honey, why don't you keep our food warm in the oven, and I'll be right back."

Neal suddenly did look like Gaius, the Roman general who would not be intimidated by anyone or any goddess. He continued to stare down Hel.

"Look at me," Vivien whispered calmly.

He did.

I feel in my heart of hearts no harm will come to me. Hel is concerned about something here on earth. She wants my input.

Neal's eyes widened at Vivien's ability to speak to

him with her mind. They'd been in sync and had spoken this way before, but he was getting used to the idea.

He nodded reluctantly. "Okay." Neal glanced at Hel and spoke with conviction. "If you go over five minutes, I'll find a way to hell and snatch her back myself."

Hel inclined her head in acknowledgment of Neal's threat but did not speak. She seemed to find the whole situation amusing.

Before Neal sensed Hel's mirth, Vivien moved next to the goddess. "What now?"

"Get your wine." Hel commanded.

Vivien's voice rose to a high pitch. "What?"

"You cannot eat or drink in my realm. It will connect you prematurely to the underworld." Her eyebrows raised. "Unless you'd like to stay for a while?"

Immediately Vivien grabbed her glass from the table.

Hel lifted the crimson red hood over her head. "Touch the crystal."

With one last glance at Neal, Vivien placed her palm over the top of Hel's staff, entirely covering the crystal ball.

When Vivien began flickering in and out, she hollered out to Neal, "Remember, put the food in the oven!"

****

The rich smell of pine needles greeted Vivien as her eyes fluttered open. A golden crackling fire sat ten feet away, and next to it stood a magnificent Christmas tree. Colorful blown glass and metallic ornaments hung from full branches. Some displayed Victorian scenes and others, more modern. In fact, Vivien spied one metallic colored ball portraying Santa Claus in New York City amongst Broadway marquees. Glowing yellow lights hung throughout branches, creating a glow which enchanted the tree.

Shifting her weight, Vivien realized she sat in a massive red velvet chair. Her seat became so comfortable, Vivien thought she might melt into the cushion. She took in an intimate Victorian parlor complete with a built-in carved bookshelf containing first editions opposite a semi-circular dark-wood fireplace.

Vivien never expected this. This might as well be Baker Street, and Sherlock Holmes could come through the door at any moment spouting about a new case.

Looking to her right, Vivien gazed upon Hel. She sat in another enormous red velvet chair on the other side of a small circular wood table with a thick wooden claw base. To Vivien's further amazement, her right hand still held onto that glass of merlot. It hadn't spilled.

"Is this hell?" Vivien asked in utter confusion.

Hel reached for a white teacup with red roses painted along the sides. The saucer beneath matched the cup. A tea service sat upon a silver tray, complete with white creamer and sugar bowl also adorned in red roses. A matching teapot sat at the edge of the table. "I prefer underworld." She brought the steaming cup to her lips and sipped.

"Oh, sorry." Vivien took a long drink from her wine. She didn't know where the tea had come from but thought it better not to ask. Vivien gazed upon the greenery. "Is that a living Christmas tree?"

Hel put her teacup back on its saucer. "Not at all. Nothing can live here, but I maintain the image, and I've added those little green sticks from your upper level that smell like pine."

"Nice touch." Her brows drew together as Vivien inspected the holiday tree further. "So, I'm looking at a hologram?"

At last, unhooking the crimson cloak, which still hung from her shoulders, Hel explained, "No, it is more than a hologram. In your world you would call it a 3D image."

Vivien nodded. "I see."

Hel clapped her hands. "Snowball! Sugarplum!"

Suddenly, two small beings ran into the parlor dressed as elves. They stopped in front of the fireplace and bowed to Hel. Standing three feet high with sallow rubbery skin, they resembled pudgy trolls. One wore a red coat and pointy hat trimmed in white fur, and the second wore the same only in green.

"Please bring fresh tea service."

The odd duo bowed again and moved forward. Their gaze moved up and down Vivien in surprise.

Vivien instinctively pulled back against the side of her chair, but maintained eye contact out of respect.

Hel flashed a glance at Vivien. "These are my servants."

Then she turned to Snowball and Sugarplum. "This is Boudicca in another flesh. She is visiting briefly and do not—I repeat—do not bring her any food or beverage, do you understand?"

The servants nodded spastically with large eyes above fleshy wide mouths.

"All right, then," Hel spat with finality, flicking her hand in the air.

The one in red picked up the teapot, and the creature in green took the tray. Off they ran in a blink of an eye.

Taking another slug from her wine, Vivien leveled a look at Hel. "Why do you dress them up?"

Deep rumbling almost shook the sweet parlor with Hel's laughter. "I do it for fun. But it is only seasonal." She angled the skin side of her face toward Vivien. "I'm very misunderstood, Vivien. People in your realm think I'm a monster. I actually enjoy the holiday season and love Christmas! Yes, I do. I have a role to fulfill here as goddess of the underworld, but I'm not the horror people make me out to be. I'm doing my job, just like many others."

Taking another drink from her glass, Vivien knew this night would go down as the most bizarre Christmas Eve she'd ever experienced. She placed her wine carefully onto the tabletop. "You never cease to surprise me, Hel. I feel I understand you better than I did five minutes ago."

"I'm glad."

Sugarplum and Snowball rushed back in with a brand-new tea service, and this time included miniature cranberry scones. After placing the delights in front of Hel, they bowed in unison once, turned, and marched out the door.

Once the large wooden door slammed shut, Vivien moved to the edge of her seat. "Now, why am I here, Hel? I'd really like to get back to my hot soulmate." Whether it was wine or the happy room, Vivien felt more relaxed with the woman who managed the dead.

Hel added sugar and cream to the tea she'd just poured. Stirring slowly with a small silver spoon she lifted from the tray, Hel appeared to be concentrating.

Vivien's patience began to wear thin, but she dare not press the goddess further. All she could do was wait.

After Hel took her first sip, she lowered the teacup onto the saucer.

Hel's eye turned to crystal silver with a new intensity as she peered into Vivien's soul. "I can no longer remain silent."

Vivien shuddered but attempted to cover the movement with another reach for her wine glass. She felt it necessary to take a big slug.

"I have been haunted by the same vision for the past year, and I feel you are connected to this vision."

"Uh huh." Vivien's voice came out like a squeak. She promptly cleared her throat.

Hel leaned in closer. "I see my realm filling up with bodies in an unprecedented manner. Since my dimension is endless, I can accommodate all, but my worry is that earth will be out of balance. It is not an earthly world war that brings more dead to occupy my mansions, it is because of powerful evil that I see unleashed upon your upper realm."

"What?" Vivien screamed. "Are you sure it isn't from Dagda? After all, he did try to control Earth, and many died before I defeated him at the solstice."

Hel shook her head. "No, it is another entity that is sending these souls to me."

Vivien's wine glass projected out of her hand and shattered against the mantelpiece. Rage swept through her body and mind. She'd just gotten rid of Dagda, saved her friend from Krampus, and now she had to hear another prediction of evil ready to attack.

Hel clapped her hands again, and Snowball entered with a small broom and dustpan to sweep up the broken glass.

Vivien dropped her head into her hands. Her psychic tingling running through her nervous system confirmed Hel saw a very possible future on earth.

"I'm sorry," Vivien breathed out with a wispy voice. "Go on."

Hel stopped for a moment to give Vivien some respite. "I sympathize with you, Vivien, because I do not want this future either. I prefer order and shall do whatever is needed to keep harmony and stability in my house."

Raising her head, Vivien took a long, calming breath in. "I understand."

"Unfortunately, there is not much more to my vision, except that I believe you saw one of these creatures during your recent battle."

Vivien's breathing stopped for a moment. "You mean a banshee, or shadow person? Please don't tell me it's one of those black-eyed children?"

With a wave of her hand, Hel frowned. "No, it's not one of those kids. They are so annoying. They always try to trick people into becoming one of my occupants." She zoned in on Vivien's face. "This creature is an adult female."

Sitting up straight, Vivien felt lighter. "Wait a minute. I didn't see anything female in our combat except for banshees. You just said it isn't any of them, and everything went back into that black hole that morning. We all witnessed their exile."

Hel cocked her head. "You did not see any additional otherworldly entities?"

"No! I just told you!" Vivien stopped her mouth. "Please forgive me." She exhaled. "In my own defense, I literally just saved the upper realm, so I'm a little upset. But I know you are earnest in your feelings, so can you tell me anything else?"

Hel settled back into her encircling chair and then appeared to be searching the ceiling. After a few moments, she glanced back at Vivien. "She is not on earth, but she is close by. This entity can travel through dimensions."

After a long pause, Vivien edged closer to Hel. "Anything else?"

The goddess locked eyes with Vivien. "She is ancient and extremely powerful."

Vivien bolted to the fireplace and smacked her hands onto the mantel.

Hel came up behind her. "This is not happening now." She placed a hand onto Vivien's shoulder. "I don't know when she will enter your world, and there is a slim chance she may move on. I just felt I needed to warn you."

Vivien turned. "Thank you."

Hel moved her hands onto each side of Vivien's shoulders, careful to touch only cloth. "Oh, and one more thing."

"Yes?"

"Merry Christmas!" Hel's silver eye sparkled.

Chapter Fourteen

"It's time for Christmas stockings!" Vivien happily yelped, jumping up and down.

"Yes, it is!" Chuckling, Neal followed her.

They raced into the living room like kids.

Two overstuffed stockings hung from the mantelpiece. Each sock presented their names in embroidery on red felt with white trim and a small toy elf on top. Neal had them made by a local artisan before Vivien's battle with Dagda.

Since the front window blinds had been shut and the hour still early, light billowed into the room solely from their Christmas tree. But not just light; there existed a feeling of warmth in her home. Vivien felt safe for the first time in a very long time.

Vivien reached for Neal's stocking. "Look! Santa left you something." Taking the sock off the metal mantel clip, she turned to find him right behind her.

"Why, thank you, Santa." Holding his stocking with one arm, Neal plucked Vivien's sock off the clip and gave it to her.

"Thanks."

"No, you can thank Santa." Neal led Vivien to the couch.

They sat down amongst red and gold holiday pillows.

"Of course, what was I thinking?" Vivien smacked

herself on the forehead with her palm. They had agreed two days earlier to shop for each other's stocking stuffers. But Vivien relished Neal's suspension of disbelief.

He leaned toward Vivien and whispered, "You first."

Pulling her stocking onto her lap, Vivien tugged out a handcrafted fabric white angel whose top half stuck out the top. She noticed it immediately when they entered the room. At eight inches high, with embroidered closed eyes, a smile, and small nylon net wings, the angel delighted Vivien. She embraced it to her cheek. "Thanks, Santa. I'm going to add her to my meditation room."

"Good." Neal smiled ear to ear.

"Santa has such good taste." Vivien's lips crinkled into a sideways smile, as she continued to pluck out items.

She ran through a myriad of chocolates, some in bars, and some wrapped in Santa-shaped colored foil. Vivien even pulled out classic green, red, and orange ribbon candy, and at last her favorite, maple sugar candies.

Vivien laughed in delight. "I'm going to fall into a sugar coma!"

"That's okay, hon. I'll join you!"

She broke out in guffaws and pulled out remaining holiday socks, body butters, and winter scented perfumes. The final item got lodged in the bottom of Vivien's sock. "Hang on, I need to get this one unstuck." After getting her fingers around a square object, she pulled it to the surface. Vivien held a small red velvet box.

Neal's face went pale. "No!" He snatched the box from Vivien's hand.

"What's wrong?" she asked in dismay.

He didn't answer and strode briskly past the living room entrance. After a few seconds, Neal came back with the box in hand.

"Here you go," he stated and sat down next to her.

Vivien stared at him, and he looked down. "Should I open it?"

"Yes, of course." Neal slid closer to her on the couch.

"I just wondered, because of your reaction."

Neal laid his arm behind her neck with thoughtful eyes. "Please don't intuitively focus on what just happened."

Vivien didn't realize she'd stopped breathing for a moment. Did he believe her red box held an engagement ring? Deciding not to even ask, Vivien took in a much-needed breath. "Okay."

Neal's face relaxed. "Let me just say there's a time and place for everything."

"I agree." Vivien kissed him. "Now can I open it?"

Neal nodded. "Yes, please do."

After the lid lifted, Vivien gazed upon a stunning pair of earrings in the shape of a leaping Rudolph. His red nose held a ruby and his 14-karat gold body was strewn with diamonds.

"They're beautiful!" She kissed him again.

"I thought it would be nice to have some Christmas bling to go with your classic red dress."

"I love them. I'll wear them today when everyone comes over."

Next, Neal whirled through his stocking, pulling

out a variety of socks, designer shaving kit items, candy, and finally a pair of diamond snowflake cufflinks.

He held the box of cufflinks and glanced at Vivien. "We had the same idea—holiday bling."

Vivien laughed. "Great minds think alike."

"They do. Thank you, honey." He embraced her sweetly.

****

Vivien's head rested upon Neal's shoulder.

After partaking of a sumptuous Christmas breakfast and opening gifts, they luxuriated on her living room couch. Neal lit a color log in the fireplace, and they watched yellow, gold, blue, and purple flames dance.

Their gifts sat under the tree. Vivien angled her head to look upon her presents from Neal. She planned to include the large crystal ball in her meditation room, as well as a painting of Boudicca. The Celtic warrior queen sat majestically upon a horse swirling among amber, gold, and red watercolors. Clothed in a tan animal skin tunic, leather arm bands, and deerskin boots, Boudicca held a long pewter sword extended from her right hand. Her face and arms displayed circular patterns of Celtic battle paint in red and blue, while emerald eyes mesmerized.

"I'm glad you like your little house," Vivien mumbled softly.

Neal pulled her closer, until Vivien's head rested on his chest. "I love it. I always will."

Inspiration came to Vivien months ago to have a model maker create a copy of Neal's home, including the two cypress trees on his front lawn. The model came out amazing and was set on a wooden base. Neal proclaimed he would add it to his mantelpiece.

Vivien gazed upon two glass mugs of hot mulled wine sitting on her coffee table. Crimson liquid set off a tawny glow in front of the flames, coupled with a heavenly scent of dense spices, lemon, orange, and apple.

They snatched up their mugs, and Neal clicked Vivien's glass.

They drank.

Christmas spirit had truly come to Vivien's house, a house shared with her soul partner, Neal. She wondered in the future if they would stay in her home or live in his? It was a question whose answer she looked forward to with joyful anticipation.

One more image popped into Vivien's mind, which she knew would play out in three hours upon their friends' arrival.

Vivien lifted a glass of wine amongst many other glasses to make a toast.

"I'd like to quote one of my favorite authors. So, to quote Tiny Tim from Charles Dickens' *A Christmas Carol,* 'God bless us, every one!' "

"Hear, hear!"

They all drank in honor of another day well lived in a world without a Christmas demon.

A word about the author…

When Starra Andrews wasn't swimming in the Pacific Ocean in her hometown of Laguna Beach, California, she busied herself by writing fantasy stories and acting on stage. Having grown up watching Rod Serling's Twilight Zone and Night Gallery shows on TV, Starra quickly fell in love with paranormal tales with a message of wisdom and love. Also, being a fan of romance novels and non-fiction ghost stories, she decided to marry the two and write paranormal novels of suspense, adventure, and intrigue with a strong romantic foundation. The sense of adventure inside her came from summers of camping with her family in Mexico (Baja California) and walking along beaches with no other footprints but hers, as her family members unpacked the camper and got ready to collect clams right off the shoreline for dinner. After attaining a B.A. degree in Theatre from University of California, Irvine, and a Professional Acting Certificate from LACC Acting Academy, an idea sparked for interviewing actors to help student actors entering the theatre arena. Starra's non-fiction book The Pursuit of Acting; Working Actors Share Their Experience and Advice was published by Praeger Publishers. Then, her paranormal short story A Hasty Decision appeared in the online magazine for speculative fiction Aberrant Dreams, and when Llewellyn Worldwide Publishers asked for real paranormal encounter stories for their Scary Story Contest, she won first place. Starra is also a member of the International Thriller Writers, which host the Thrillerfest writers conference each year in NYC. Her heroine, psychic/paranormal cleanser Vivien

Kelly and her team are in a race to rid the modern world of deadly Celtic creatures in her book trilogy, The Kelly Society. Bay of Darkness is the first book of the series. The beautiful Hudson Valley in upstate New York is where Starra now calls home. She loves being a quick train ride from New York City, but also enjoys country life. Her two tabby cats Audrey Hepburn and Vivien Leigh are her constant writing companions, and love to curl up on the table next to her laptop.